OUT ON THE PISTE

GW00493294

a novel by

DANANN SWANTON

SILVERDART
MMXIV

Published by Silverdart Ltd
Woodmancote Manor, Cirencester
Gloucestershire GL7 7ED
United Kingdom
www.silverdart.co.uk
Tel: +44 (0) 1285 831 789
enquiries@silverdart.co.uk

ISBN-13   978 0 9554581 7 0

For Geraldine and Cillian – for believing in me.

PROLOGUE

Eimear had been home all of five minutes and already, her family were driving her mad. Had her three brothers always been so loud? Did her mum really have to nag her for leaving her suitcase strewn across the floor the moment she stepped through the front door? Had her father always laughed so uproariously at his own jokes, especially when no one else found them funny?

They hadn't seen each other for five months so Eimear had expected it would have taken longer than it actually had for the excitement of being reunited to wear off and for the normal irritation of family life to resume. But no, they were as mental as always and it took all of minutes for Eimear to be reminded of it.

In the overly crowded kitchen of her family home, her youngest brother accidentally knocked over some glasses. As they smashed across the floor, Eimear welcomed the diversion and slipped out to escape to her room. All of her uncles, aunties and cousins had come over to welcome her home from her ski season in France. While she was really touched by their warmth and was happy to see them, she knew that it took little excuse for them to get together and have a party. Even as she had slipped out of the kitchen, she had seen her uncle reach into the liquor cabinet for whatever spirit he could get his hand on. The party had begun.

She stepped over her two older brothers who were wrestling on the stairs ("You are both morons! Move outta my way!"), reached the first floor and pushed open her bedroom door. It was so weird to see it again after so long. The girl who stood in the doorway now was nothing like the girl who had slept there badly five months ago, so sick was she with nerves the night before she left. Eimear walked into her room and lay down on the bed. Various boy bands looked down at her from the wall and her childhood teddies welcomed her back from the shelves. To her, they were now a symbol of the innocence that, thanks to her five months in France, had gone.

1

France. She smiled a bitter sweet smile as she thought about it. It was so weird that no one under her roof could understand what she had just been through, what she had left behind.

Needing to talk to someone who would get it, she fished her Irish phone, now reunited with her after so long, from her pocket, and messaged Michelle.

Miss you already.

When can we leave again?

The response came back instantaneously.

Please God, soon!!!!

Eimear smiled. Now that they both had the taste of freedom, she had a feeling there would be a fair few more adventures for her and her friend. Feeling exhaustion take over her, she closed her eyes, snuggled up to her favourite old toy and dreamed of France.

CHAPTER 1

Eimear bolted upright, froze in her seat and then furtively glanced around the classroom. She had been doing it again. The thing they were not supposed to do. That wicked, ill-disciplined, forbidden 'D' word. Daydreaming. And this time, her illicit act was made so much worse by the content of her dream, especially since she was in Religious education, the very lesson where they were taught that such dreams were mortal sins. She had been focusing on Sister Hilda's voice drone on about the Ten Commandments and then those prohibited, predatory, sex-obsessed, alien creatures had crept into her mind. The sort of creatures every mother warned their daughters about and every father hoped their daughters never touched. Boys. She and her classmates had been told by the nuns and other teachers in their school that they should not ever fantasise about the male species, let alone touch them. Or at least not until they had grown up and had married the boy their ma had suggested.

The rain trickled down outside of the classroom window, creating a curtain of condensation on the inside of the glass. Eimear cleared a gap in the moisture, leant her forehead against the window and watched the rain drops collect in muddy puddles in the playground in an attempt to distract herself from her thoughts. In the distance, she could see a class of first years running around the hockey pitch and snorted with glee at the sight of the drowned and bedraggled girls. Suddenly, she wished she was running around the hockey pitch too; Fr. Joseph always said the best way to purge one's soul of sinful thought was to hit the exercise and sweat it all out. Mind you, Eimear thought, Fr. Joseph might just be suggesting the girls dressed up in their gym kit and got all sweaty as he enjoyed watching that sort of thing, if what the papers said was to be believed. Eimear shook herself in disgust. Snap out of it, she thought. Thinking of boys was bad enough; accusing her school and village priest of being a pervert was far, far worse.

She knew what was going to happen next; that unwelcome

emotion all Catholics in the world are no stranger to was going to arrive, much like a despised family member at the annual Christmas party. Guilt. Catholic bloody guilt. As expected, it materialised within seconds and, as always, hit Eimear like a ton of bricks. As she started beating herself up for thinking such despicable thoughts and convincing herself that her future was to be one of eternal damnation, she glanced at the clock at the front of the classroom. Eimear's mood darkened further when she realised she still had the second half of double religious education to get through. Disgruntled by life, she returned her forehead to her resting place on the window to continue chastising herself whilst watching the growing puddles and miserable first years running across the muddy field.

Eimear and the rest of the pupils who attended St. Mary's School for Girls were no strangers to Catholic guilt. In fact, it seemed to be the basis of their education. The nuns and teachers thrived on telling the girls they needed to beg for forgiveness from God if they so much as forgot to flush the toilet after peeing. But when it came to the shameful, disreputable topic of sex, the nuns had a field day. School taught the girls that the only contraception was to say no, that sex did not exist outside of marriage and that they were doomed to eternal damnation if they were so much as seen with a member of the opposite sex outside of the school gates. Condoms, when found in an older brother's drawer, were mistaken for, and used as, extra powerful water bombs. Family planning clinics were places families went to decide the best day care for their child. Casual sex was the description used for married couples 'doing it' on a lazy Sunday morning. STDs? Were they a new band to recently emerge from America that none of the girls had heard of yet? Eimear was moulded by a Catholic girls school and God Almighty, those girls were aware of the absence of men on a daily basis. Desperation oozed out of every school girl's pores; an obese sixty-year-old builder, whose daily attire incorporated baggy trousers, revealing an unattractive and hairy butt crack, could walk through school and the perfumes were being whipped out of the school bags and make-up applied so thickly, it would have to be removed with a chisel. Eimear's main sex education (other than the cartoon book her parents handed to her as a four-year-old child to explain why her mother had suddenly grown a particularly large bump) was from those in the school who were daring and rebellious enough to have 'done IT'. Eimear would huddle in the back of her Chemistry lessons where she shared a work bench with Ciara O'Donnell, a notorious slag. Amongst the Bunsen burners and science goggles, whilst keeping an eye out for their teacher, those in earshot of Ciara would listen to the stories of her latest experiments with the prohibited opposite sex. She would throw out various moves she had practised such as, 'The Wheelbarrow' or 'Doggy' at the inexperienced who nodded as though they understood what she was talking about whilst secretly cursing their naivety for thinking a wheelbarrow was nothing more than a means of transport for compost.

As Eimear and her friends got older, they despised their innocence more and more so would try to be rebellious whenever the opportunity arose. Eimear would tell the latest boy on the scene to wait down the road just a few metres away from the gate because that was what a real revolutionary did. Some of the more daring friends in her circle even attempted the taboo activity – kissing boys. The really radical girls amongst her group followed the footsteps of Ciara O'Donnell and did go further. But no matter how daring or rebellious Eimear and her friends were, none of them could ever escape the warning words of the head of religious education – "You can hide from me but you can't hide from God!"

This sentence was shouted at them every Tuesday morning after they had been dragged out of their mass-avoiding hiding place. Eimear and her friends would pile into a toilet cubicle, place one foot on the toilet seat and wedge the other one against the wall in order to fit as many people as possible around the toilet bowl. They would all snigger silently as they thought they had outwitted everyone and therefore, avoided having to listen to Fr. Joseph drone on for the next hour. But, alas, they were not quick enough for the head of R.E. who had an uncanny knack of knowing which particular cubicle they had chosen as their hiding place each week. As Eimear squished on the toilet seat in between Cathleen O'Donovan and Siobhan Ryan amongst a number of other girls from her form, a much feared head would suddenly appear underneath the door. A public toilet floor was no place for a woman of sixty-odd years yet this teacher was committed to getting those mass-avoiding heathens to the chapel no matter what in order to save their lost souls. As the girls were all marched out of the cubicle one by one, that fateful line was shouted at them. Hearing that sentence so many times can cause serious psychological damage to a young girl and it slowly became the voice of Eimear's conscience any time she was doing 'inappropriate things' with an 'inappropriate person'.

As Eimear and her friends grew older, they would all try and shrug off the damning voice of their R.E. teacher. Eimear thought she was safe, hidden away from school in the bedroom of some boy and would start to relax and feel a bit daring. How brave and rebellious she was, to be alone in a room with a real boy! Yet she could not enjoy her courageous move for long; when she least expected it, that damning line would start booming around her head in the austere Northern Irish tones of her teacher. Next thing, she would picture God bobbing on his cloud in the corner of the bedroom, shaking his head in disappointment and disgust. Jesus Christ, Eimear would think, there is really nothing more off-putting when you are getting a little bit familiar with a guy than having an audience, especially when that audience is God.

By the time Eimear was eighteen, she had had enough, enough of allowing the guilt to ruin her life and enough of the oppression. She decided she needed to leave Ireland, escape from the guilt and travel. What she needed most, she decided, was to have a gap year before she went off to University. Most importantly, she needed to ensure that the object of her year off was to be inundated with men. Lots and lots of men. It was only by leaving the country that she would succeed in ridding herself of the image of God hanging over her shoulder, watching every incriminating gesture, conversation or kiss. In her final year of school,

Eimear's friend Michelle revealed that she was going travelling to a ski resort after completion of her Leaving Cert. On enquiring if there would be any boys there and hearing the response 'lots of them', Eimear made her decision. She finished her exams, packed her bags, told her family she was going to live in France to 'find herself' and got on a plane to Geneva.

In the month of December, the two friends from school embarked on a plane which would take them away from their friends and family for five months, away from Christmas at home and from English-speaking locals. As the plane left Cork airport runway, Eimear found herself whispering a nervous 'Hail Mary' to subvert the haunting thought that she was hurtling through the air in an over-sized, glorified tin can which, knowing her luck, would plummet to the ground, resulting in her imminent death. Well, I guess there are some religious habits I won't be able to shake, she told herself as she glanced out the window at the increasingly small landscape which had been the home she had known so well for so many years. As the plane climbed higher and higher, Eimear hoped she had made the right decision. Most importantly, Eimear hoped she would finally put her guilt behind her and find a man who would succeed in titillating her mind and body without the voice of the Head of Religious Education creeping into her brain.

And so the plane soared through the sky, bringing her one step closer towards the magical little ski resort called L'Homme in the beautiful French Alps.

CHAPTER 2

Eimear was not the most agile or graceful of young women. In fact, she could barely walk in a straight line without tripping over her feet. Her family, not known for their sensitivity, nick-named her 'Bambi' at a young age and, as she grew older, she gave them more reason rather than less to keep this mocking but affectionate pet name. Sports were not her forte; whilst her brothers had raced out of the door every weekend, with rugby kit, hurling equipment and Gaelic footballs in tow, Eimear had preferred to curl up on the sofa with a good book. Her parents, both runners, would casually drop heart attack statistics and obesity warnings into conversations when in her hearing range in the hope that putting the fear of fatness and imminent death into her would spur her on to do some exercise. On the rare occasion that Eimear decided to humour her family and attempt some exercise, she would convince herself after ten minutes that the pounding heart and lack of breath was a sign of some serious, crippling disease which was only being aggravated further by pushing her body too hard. She would quickly return to the couch-potato lifestyle with books in tow much to her family's despair, leaving them believing anxiously that their only daughter and sister would be torn from them in some freak accident caused by lack of movement.

As for skiing, the sport had never even crossed Eimear's mind until it became a 'get out of Ireland free' card, thus an excuse to leave home. Needless to say, West Cork's small hills had never seemed like the appropriate place to start throwing oneself down a mountain on sticks.

The plane rose above the clouds and Eimear's mind strayed onto the sport she would learn and hopefully master over the next five months. So excited was she of the prospect of moving to a new town which was apparently inundated with the opposite sex, she had not given her inability to ski much thought, nor had it manifested itself as much of a problem on the rare occasion her mind had drifted onto the subject. The voice of an air hostess informed all passengers that they could now leave their seats if they wished; the sound of the unclipping seat belts rang throughout the cabin and Eimear started giving skiing some serious thought. She imagined the whole experience to be somewhat similar to the skiing scene in the second Bridget Jones film. Eimear considered herself to be far more competent than Bridget in life itself so did not think mastering skiing would be a problem. After all, even after a messy and undignified mountain descent, the inadequate Bridget still managed to get down the slope on her first attempt whilst not breaking any bones. Eimear did not see why she would be any different and immediately, her confidence soared. I bet I will be flying down the most complicated of slopes with style and poise by the end of my first week, she declared to herself with extreme certainty and a grin.

Eimear leaned back in her chair, found her favourite album on her iPod, placed her headphones in her ears and closed her eyes. Within seconds she was dreaming of her upcoming ski adventure in which she too, like Bridget Jones, found her own Mr Darcy. In this particular scenario, she discovered her dream man on the ski slope after she had fallen over in the snow, gently and with dignity of course.

As she lay on the soft, white, mountain top looking vulnerable yet sexy and seductive, a large, burly, muscular ski instructor would ski past and immediately swoop to her rescue. She envisaged him removing her from the snow drift she had tenderly bumped into, and as he carried her down the slope, he whispered into her ear that she was the most beautiful woman he had ever seen, even when covered in snow with bits of foliage in her hair and could he please take her out for dinner? Eimear snorted to herself as she pictured her chivalrous rescue; but as quickly as her dream man had saved her, this picture was replaced with an image of her lying in a hospital bed in a full body cast surrounded by French-speaking nurses. Fear replaced her initial excitement at the hope of finding her man in such romantic settings as the reality that any falls could (and Eimear had a slight inkling that they probably would) result in every bone in her body breaking rather than picking up a hunky man. She decided the best way to avoid breakages would be to avoid falling over at all costs both in reality or in her dream world, even if it did mean missing out on the opportunity of being rescued by Monsieur Stud Muffin.

Worried that she would be a complete ignoramus on arrival in Geneva, Eimear turned to Michelle to question her about what she should expect. Michelle's family were far more travelled than Eimear's and she found herself to be slightly in awe of how worldly Michelle really seemed to be. She was an experienced skier and had been on various ski holidays since she was a young child. Seeing her as some sort of skiing guru, Eimear started bombarding her friend with question after question; soon, she wished she hadn't.

Michelle started explaining about the grading of ski runs, from blue (easiest) to black (hardest), snow ploughing, something called moguls which were apparently mounds of snow one 'hopped' over, a type of ski called 'twin tips', helmets, jumps and the option of skiing both on and off the piste. (Eimear had initially thought Michelle was discussing how easily it was to get 'pissed' until she explained that piste meant ski slope. Eimear decided to keep that little misunderstanding to herself.) With each new detail, Eimear lost a shade of colour from her face until soon, even Michelle noticed there was a problem.

"What's up?"

"Michelle… am I going to die?" Eimear asked, her voice barely audible over the din of the cabin.

"Well…" her friend thought for a moment, too long for Eimear's liking, and with a nonchalant shrug said, "you could, but you probably won't. You are more likely to die in the bus on the way up the mountain than on a ski run." Michelle obviously thought she was helping the situation. She really wasn't.

Eimear clutched her friend's arm with panic. "I didn't think this through. I can't ski, what am I doing? I am the most accident-prone person I know! For God sake! This is it, my life is over. I am going to die at the age of eighteen. Oh my God, I am going to die a virgin! I want to go home. I am getting the next available return flight back to Ireland. I should never have left, me with my ideas of interesting exotic French skiing men, stupid stupid girl. Do you know what? When I die from falling over the side of a cliff, it will be religious karma getting its own back because I had lustful thoughts before marriage. I am telling you, the nuns warned us! I should just have stayed at home and married one of the local farmer's sons!"

"Get a grip woman!" Michelle, who did not have much patience at the best of times, shook her friend with a fair amount of force. "You will not die, you most certainly will not die a virgin and you really need to pull yourself together if you are willing to settle for those local boys. There are some seriously fit men in ski resorts, you should not give up that easily; I thought you had more balls than this!" Michelle was not only experienced in skiing but was also no stranger to the opposite sex.

"And if I don't die, I will most likely kill someone!" Unfortunately, Eimear's rising hysteria had led to a significant increase in volume; the din from surrounding passengers decreased dramatically on hearing this statement. Michelle had to give her friend a serious dig in the ribs to encourage her to shut the hell up.

Lowering her voice slightly, Eimear continued, "I am going to accidentally feed someone raw chicken, give them salmonella, kill them and spend the rest of my life in prison. Then, who knows what I might pick up! Those who were once heterosexual quickly become lesbians when forced to live in confined spaces. Michelle, I just would not be a good lesbian. I mean, I don't think I would. I have never been with a man so maybe I am a lesbian but I would like to be able to find that out naturally rather than become one by being a victim of circumstance!"

There was a stunned silence after this diatribe.

"Eimear, please calm down. I may need to slap you to bring you back to your senses if you do not do so quickly. You are probably not a lesbian but if you are one, as much as I love you, please give me warning before you bring someone back to our new accommodation so I can make plans to avoid witnessing your lesbian activity. As for the salmonella fear, we were not put through our paces at Alpine Cookery School for nothing. So, as I have already told you, get a grip. Now."

An air hostess's voice crackled over the tannoy system. "Ladies and Gentlemen, we are about to start descending into Geneva airport. Please put up your trays, fasten your seat belts and turn off all electronic equipment. Thank you."

An air hostess appeared by their side and swept the various Pringle boxes and sweet wrappers into rubbish bags. The two girls clipped their trays into place and sat back in their seats in preparation for the descent. Eimear, confidence majorly diminished, plonked her forehead against the plastic cabin window and started rotating her face as far as possible in an attempt to see as much of the new landscape as physically feasible.

"Where is this ski resort anyway?" Eimear asked after a few minutes, her previously whimpering voice now held a note of curiosity.

"Jesus Em, have you never looked at a map?"

"You know geography is not my finest subject Michelle and I never read any books about ski resorts so I only have you as my basis of knowledge!" Eimear stuttered in defence of her ignorance.

"There is geographical knowledge which one may gain from studying the subject. However, there is also something called common sense; you decide to live in a new country, you do some research. I suggest you look into acquiring that important virtue some time soon." Michelle was clearly getting tired of the amount of hand holding her friend required.

Eimear returned her gaze to the window and decided she really needed to get herself in gear if she was to survive the season. She had already deteriorated into a pathetic panicking mess and the plane had not even landed yet.

As the plane screeched along the runway, bringing Eimear one step closer to her new home for five months, she made herself a promise. She crossed every flexible limb and swore she would not make a fool of herself this season; she would defy all of her friends' and family's suspicions that she was a bit of a ditz. She would master skiing and she would conquer the French language. She would learn to drive on the wrong side of the road and in the snow. She would be the most fantastic cook in the history of chalet hosts and leave every surface in her chalet so clean one could eat their food off of it. She would wine and dine her guests and every single one would beg to stay for another week. She would not make mistakes, she would not break a bone and she would not give any one food poisoning. She would find herself a man, maybe even have a bit of a fling and end the season STD and pregnancy free. She would probably not become a lesbian.

As the plane hit the tarmac, the young eighteen-year-old girl with a new, fierce determination started collecting her belongings together in preparation for disembarking the plane and embarking on the next chapter of her life.

CHAPTER 3

Eimear walked through the baggage collection exit and was instantly greeted by hordes of happy, eagerly awaiting faces in the arrival lounge. She glanced from face to face in search of her new employers and cast her mind back to the first time she met them, an occasion which had been both successful and somewhat embarrassing.

She and Michelle had flown to London for their interviews with the chalet company bosses Ian and Lucy Johnson who had requested that they interview each of the girls both individually and as a couple. Should they employ the two girls, they would be expected to run a chalet together. Their prospective employers needed to check their conversational skills were intact and assess whether they could work together, or if they would be likely to kill each other once the going got tough.

Eimear, who had won the first interview by beating Michelle's rock with paper in their fool-proof decision-making process, 'Rock, Paper, Scissors', pushed open the door of a swanky London bar and searched for the couple. Looking around at the tightly-fitted designer-labelled suits propping up the bar, sipping mochas and reading the Financial Times, she thought over the phone call she had received from Lucy the night before.

Before hanging up the phone, the prospective new boss had said,

"I am looking forward to meeting you and your boyfriend. See you tomorrow, have a safe flight."

Before Eimear had even had a chance to register what had been said, the sound of the disconnected phone call rang out through her hand set.

Maybe I misheard, Eimear had thought, as she had spotted a tanned couple at a table beside the large window, ski magazines spread out before them.

"So, how do we say your name exactly?" Eimear was asked by Lucy after introductions had been made, hands had been shaken and Eimear had taken a seat, "Is it like the bird, Emu?"

"It is sort of like the bird, but replace the 'u' with an 'er'. So you say it 'Eemer'."

"So, Eimear, how long have you and your boyfriend been together, Mitch is it?" Lucy queried.

"My who?"

"Your boyfriend Mitch." Meeting a blank look, she continued, "the one you will be doing your season with?"

Suddenly flustered, Eimear responded,

"Oh, you mean Michelle! She isn't my boyfriend, she is a girl, she's my girlfriend. I must have confused you when I called her Mitch, that is my nickname for her. It should have said her name on her CV though?" she asked, now confused.

Lucy's and Ian's eyes darted to one another then shot back to Eimear, curiosity evident in their look.

"She's not my girlfriend in the girlfriend sense!" Eimear exclaimed, a little too loudly. "I meant she is a friend who is a girl. We aren't lesbians, at least I don't think, whoever knows these days." She laughed awkwardly. "She is my friend from school, we grew up together."

The Johnsons' faces looked puzzled.

However, now that identities, genders and sexual preferences were established, the interview continued well, or so Eimear thought. Lucy asked most of the questions.

As Eimear was discussing the importance of customer service, she stole a quick look in Ian's direction. Her prospective boss appeared to be in some sort of discomfort. His face, which had been a normal shade when Eimear had met him, was now bright red and he looked embarrassed about something. After a few more furtive glances in his direction, she noticed that the cause of his discomfort seemed to be her. Ian's eyes repeatedly flickered towards an area beneath her neck, then to the ceiling in an attempt to avoid looking at something, but his eyes kept returning to the same spot.

Flummoxed, Eimear could not think what the problem was. She was starting to feel somewhat uncomfortable by the attention she was getting and feared that the man in front of her was a bit odd.

When the interview eventually drew to an end, she shook hands with the couple. Discomfort aside, she was confident that she had nailed the interview and, as long as Michelle didn't cock it up, the job would be theirs.

Walking outside to tag-team her friend, Eimear noticed a few more bemused glances in her direction from passers-by. Michelle, who had been waiting anxiously in the bar next door, took one look at her, let out an almighty snort and pointed at her friend's top. Glancing down, Eimear saw that a newly-missing top button revealed her once white, now yellow, aging, lucky Marks and Spencer double-A-cup bra for the whole world to see. Mortification had flooded every inch of her body as she realised the cause of Ian's discomfort.

The man wasn't odd at all, nor did he have a nervous twitch as Eimear had thought. The poor man could just see her lady lumps and was scared of being called a pervert if caught staring at her breasts.

"Jesus Christ, Eimear!" Michelle started hysterically laughing. "They will think we are desperate hookers who like to entice prospective employers by flashing them!"

"Oh, and they think we are lesbians. So we are desperate lesbian hookers," Eimear sniffed.

Michelle's laughter evaporated; with a sigh of frustration, she raised her eyes to heaven, uttered a string of blasphemous swear words and marched into the bar with an air of a knight coming to his fair damsel's rescue.

Maybe Ian and Lucy had, after all liked the aging bra. Maybe they had loved Michelle's personality enough to realise that, if they were to hire her, Eimear had to come too as she was unfortunately part of the package. Maybe they just preferred Michelle's voluptuous double-D cups which she managed to contain within her top.

Or perhaps the two girls had salvaged the situation by showing that they would survive the season without killing one another in their joint interview (Eimear had found a cardigan with which to cover her humble and exposed cleavage).

Whatever their reasons, the Johnsons had liked the girls

enough in spite of bras and gender confusion to offer them the jobs the following day.

As Eimear dragged her luggage through the doors into the arrival area, she hoped that this memory which still caused her much embarrassment would not repeat itself. Just to be on the safe side, she checked all buttons were correctly fastened and added an extra jumper and her ski jacket.

One could never be too cautious, she decided, don't want to leave my breasts exposed for all of the arrival section of Geneva airport to see and it is bound to be freezing when we get outside.

Breasts safely contained, Eimear looked around the crowded arrivals area. Suddenly, Michelle dropped her numerous skis and started waving frantically. Following her line of vision, Eimear saw Lucy and Ian emerge from a circle of people and make their way towards them. Eimear could not help but think that her new bosses looked super cool; both Lucy and Ian were in their late forties, had amazing figures and had a healthy, glowing tan which radiated from their faces and arms, all of which Eimear attributed to their mountain lifestyle.

Glancing at the amount of exposed flesh on their upper body, she could not help but notice that neither of them seemed to be wrapped up in ski gear. Instead, Ian had a leather jacket slung over his arm and cool sunglasses perched on the top of his head while Lucy was wearing a mini skirt, boots and a small strap top. Slightly puzzled, Eimear started wondering whether she had been too keen when she had dressed up for arctic conditions, but quickly assumed that Ian and Lucy were used to the cold so did not need to take the same precautions as a first-timer. As the two girls approached them, the couple grabbed them both and planted two kisses on their faces, one on each cheek. When Ian leant down to give Eimear a kiss on the cheek, she noticed that he hesitated slightly, giving her a quick once over and looked relieved when he noticed she was well covered.

"You are living the French culture now guys, two kisses are a must. Welcome!" Lucy gave them a huge grin and then hugged them both tightly. "Come on over and meet the rest of the team." With that, their cases were quickly removed from their grasps and they were hurtled along to join the small group of people Lucy and Ian had been hidden behind earlier.

Eimear smiled at each member of the group as introductions were made. There were three couples who would be working alongside Eimear and Michelle, all of whom appeared to be much older than they were. Leanne and Andrew, both English, were 30 years old and had left their jobs as dentists to travel the world. They had planned to work at various stages of their trip and their first stop was chalet hosts in France.

Next up were Rory, 27, and Ruth, 26, from Scotland; Rory was a budding musician but had hit a slight snag in his career in that no one seemed to want to buy his music. He and Ruth, a web designer, had decided to escape real life for a while and complete an item on their bucket list – do a ski season.

Finally, the girls were introduced to Emma, 23, and Mark, 24, from Wales. These two had not long completed their Masters degrees and, instead of finding jobs to justify spending so much money on their education, they had decided to prolong their late adolescence, delay joining the real world and do a ski season.

Each couple would run their own chalet on behalf of the company and there were four chalets in total. Eimear looked around at the new, smiling, hopeful faces and felt like she was back at her first day in school. Feeling extremely nervous all of a sudden, she hoped that she would get on well with these people who she would be living with for the next five months. Through her youthful eyes, she thought they all looked so wise and cool and hoped that she would not show herself up as a young kid in front of them.

Introductions made, the new team grabbed their belongings and made their way to the exits. When Eimear approached the doors, she squeezed her eyes shut and braced herself for the cold and snowy conditions on the other side. Clutching Michelle's arm for guidance, she gingerly stepped through the sliding doors, paused and waited for the ice cold air to hit her. And waited. Then waited some more. Nothing. No cold air, no freezing bones, no goose bumps, nothing.

"My ski gear really is amazing!" she thought, and opened her eyes to gaze upon the snow.

There was no snow. Not a smidgeon. Not a flake or icicle in sight. To Eimear's dismay, the December sunshine was surprisingly warm and people were walking around in short-sleeve tops. Lucy and Ian's choice of clothing suddenly became apparent. They were no more 'hard core' than she was, they had merely checked the weather forecast before dressing themselves. Feeling like a fool in her Michelin man outfit, Eimear opened her mouth to voice her concern, but caught a warning look from Michelle and quickly closed her mouth again. She shuffled after the retreating backs of her new colleagues, dragging her cases behind her.

While Ian threw her luggage in the boot of one of the vans, Eimear scrambled across the chairs to get the window seat beside Michelle and started peeling off her layers. The bang of a closed boot signified their near departure. Ian hopped into the driving seat and the van started reversing out of the car park. Eimear felt excitement rising, they were on their way.

CHAPTER 4

Unusually for Eimear, she did not participate with the many conversations surrounding her as the mini-bus ascended the mountain, but pressed her nose against the window in an attempt to take in everything she saw. They crossed the border from Switzerland into France and the Swiss city landscape turned into the French alpine mountain scenery, heightening her anticipation of what was to come. From the moment they had left Geneva airport, she had been trying to imagine her new alpine home and once again, she had based her ideas on films. This time, the Disney classic, 'Beauty and the Beast' had been her muse. She had envisaged French locals leaning out of their picturesque-shuttered windows calling 'Bonjour' to each other whilst chomping on their fresh, warm baguettes as the early morning sun rose over the Alps. The bus climbed further up the mountain and she struggled to contain her excitements and nerves as she realised that she too was soon to be a baguette-holding, bonjour-greeting local who jabbered away in fluent French.

Eventually, they could see a small town in the near distance and approached a sign which read 'Bienvenue à L'Homme'. The chatter of happy voices rose as everyone leaned over to the windows to observe their new town. After a few minutes of driving through increasingly populated roads, the bus pulled up outside a large chalet, one of the company's largest they were informed. The team were to live there whilst they were trained by both Ian and Lucy before being moved into their staff accommodation. Eimear stepped out of the bus and gazed around at her new alpine environment. Unlike Geneva, much to her relief, there was no shortage of snow here and she was glad she had her many layers of clothes with her after all. A snowball to the back of the head jolted her out of her reverie and the team spent a few minutes racing around the bus in what progressed into a furious snowball fight.

Once her body had taken a battering and she could stand it no more, Eimear slumped breathlessly into the nearest snow mound and from there, she observed her new home. She congratulated Disney on portraying such an accurate depiction of a typical French alpine town. Everywhere she looked, she could see quaint wooden chalets with snow-covered rooftops. Gazing up at the surrounding buildings, she saw that all of the windows were accompanied by decorative wooden shutters with designs of small hearts, flowers or deer carved into them. It was not uncommon for most chalets to have a garage on the lower ground, a place she assumed was a storage facility for skis, gear and firewood, whilst the second level was where the living area began. Many chalets had whole walls made of glass, giving the occupants breath-taking views of the nearby mountains and in most cases, outside these windows, were balconies. Eimear noticed these with particular glee; it looked as though her preconceived idea of hanging over the balcony and calling "salut" to her neighbours while holding her warm baguette under her arm was becoming more of a reality.

Once her breath had returned to her, Eimear heaved herself out of the snowdrift and left her snow angel-making colleagues to explore around the outside of the chalet further. She reached the back and she gave a little squeal of excitement; much to her delight, the chalet had a jacuzzi! She glanced around to see if anyone was looking and, noticing that her colleagues were still around the front of the chalet making various shapes in the snow, lifted up the lid and stuck her hand in to see how hot it was in the hope that Ian and Lucy may let them all get in later that evening in a gesture of goodwill.

She quickly regretted ever touching the water; the sub-zero conditions within dispelled all illusions she had. She quickly retracted her hand and promised herself that the moment the jacuzzi was functioning as it should, she would take a sneaky dip in it. She looked around at the neighbouring chalets and realised that this chalet was not alone in its ownership of a jacuzzi. In front of the other chalets, jacuzzis of all shapes and sizes nestled amongst the snow drifts. Eimear hoped the chalet she would be in charge of would have one too so that she and Michelle could throw a huge party, inviting the loads of friends they were sure to make throughout the season. Everyone would look highly sophisticated and cool whilst sipping champagne in her very own hot tub and because of this party alone, both she and Michelle would be the socialites of the town.

Eimear could picture herself lying amongst the bubbles, looking sexy in a brand new bikini, body toned and muscular from a hard day on the slopes and of course, it would be at this moment that her hunky French ski instructor would show up. He would take one look at her and say 'Eeeemur, I 'eard you were 'ere. I 'ave been looking for you. May I join you?' He would peel off his ski jacket, revealing a tight rugby jersey underneath. This would be quickly ripped off to show a toned stomach and into the hot tub he would jump and....

A cough interrupted the thought stream. Michelle had come looking for friend and appeared somewhat bemused in finding her submerged up to her thighs in a snow drift, soaked hand limp by her side and looking as though her head was amongst the clouds. Eimear, embarrassed at being caught and relieved that her friend could not see the action in her head, shook off the goose pimples which had appeared on her arm, more from imagining the muscles on her imaginary man than the cold. She returned the lid to its correct place on the hot tub, spun three hundred and sixty degrees to see as much as possible and headed back to join her new friends.

There was a flurry of activity at the front of the chalet. Frivolities finished with, everyone was transferring their luggage from the front of the van to the chalet. Eimear joined her colleagues and when the van was empty, she took a moment to gaze further afield to other parts of the town.

All of a sudden, the excitement which had been increasing second by second, drained from her. Eimear felt her knees go weak and she grabbed Michelle's arm for support. Her eyes had drifted to the edge of the town and had wandered over one of the mountains. Noticing that a significantly wide area down the centre of the mountain appeared to be particularly straight and well cared for, her eyes had drifted further up the mountain where she had seen chairs suspended from wires. It was only once her head had craned fully backwards and her eyes had reached the top of the mountain peak that she realised she had just seen her first ski run. It looked like a sheer, steep, vertical drop. Further visions and premonitions of returning home within the month in a full body cast and with a life-long phobia of all winter sports flittered through Eimear's mind. Her head swum and she squeezed Michelle's hand for comfort as she tried to steady her shaking legs.

Michelle, seeing what Eimear was looking at, grabbed her arms and faced her.

"Eimear, so help me God, you need to start relaxing more. I have told you once and will not tell you again, you probably will not die. Do you really think I would let you when it would mean I would have to be alone in the chalet cooking for all of those guests by myself? Do not be a fool! Now come on, everyone else has gone inside, let's go and mingle with the team."

Eimear gave herself a little shake; forget it now, she told herself sternly in the hope that she would be able to remove the horrific sight she had just witnessed from her memory. She had one last glance at the mountain, swallowed the lump in her throat and followed her friend inside.

CHAPTER 5

Eimear and Michelle had explored the chalet, an exact replica of the one they would be working in which was situated across the town, in excited awe. It was beautiful. There was wood everywhere. The downstairs living area was open plan and created an amazing feeling of space, warmth and comfort. After stepping through the entrance hall, the girls were met with the dining area; a funky graphic design of a cow chewing on a daisy overlooked a long, wooden farm-style table and chairs with high backs were pushed neatly underneath. A vintage-looking wooden cabinet stood to the side of the table and in it, the girls found crockery sets, cutlery, mats and coasters. The glistening kitchen was to the right hand side of the dining area, separated from it only by an island on which the girls could work.

An intimidating steel-plated hob was to the back of the kitchen and on every other kitchen surface, an array of steel gadgets and tools could be seen. Underneath a window was a sink and Eimear thought that at least she would have something interesting to look out at whilst she completed the most mind-numbingly dumb task in the world – washing up. That was until she spotted the dishwasher and felt a small surge of joy; she would be stuffing every utensil and pot used into that bad boy. She decided not to waste too much time looking around the kitchen; in her opinion, kitchens were pretty much there to serve the same purpose and, as she had seen one before, she didn't expect this one would throw up any new, exciting surprises.

On the far side of the dining area was the 'snug', a space laden with comfy chairs, sofas, beanbags and the fluffiest sheep-skin rug Eimear had ever set her eyes on. She tenderly put her foot on it and let out a satisfied sigh as it disappeared from sight, sinking into the cloud-like softness. Another old-looking chest lay against the far wall and on it and in it were various electronic gadgets including a TV, a DVD player and a sound system including an iPod docking station. Bookshelves lined the opposite section of the same wall and on it, the girls found a variety of books, DVDs and games for the guests to entertain themselves with. Most impressively, in Eimear's and Michelle's opinion at least, a beautiful, open, log fireplace featured in-between the wooden chest and the shelves. The fire had been lit when they arrived; as they watched the dancing, crackling flames and relaxed in its intense heat, they noticed that its presence completed the alpine, homely feeling the chalet had. Eimear looked upon the size of the flames with slight trepidation; she was not quite sure she and Michelle would be able to light theirs in quite the same way. A mere wisp of smoke would be an achievement.

Throughout the open-plan area, interesting bits of art work were scattered upon the walls, depicting the town in different seasons. It truly was a beautiful place, Eimear noticed.

To the back of the chalet was a small bedroom and communal bathroom. Not finding anything overly exciting in either one, the girls were satisfied that they had explored the bottom floor thoroughly and returned to the entrance hall to climb the stairs to the first floor and see what else awaited them.

There were three more bedrooms upstairs and the two smaller ones appeared to be set out like the one on the bottom floor. Each room had a bed which could be turned into two singles or one double depending on the guests' requirements. There was also a wardrobe and a bedside cabinet in each room and another landscape picture on the wall. Eimear didn't find any of the smaller rooms to be particularly exciting although noticed that, like the other chalets, these rooms too had cute little decorative hearts carved into the wooden shutters on the outside of the windows. The two small bedrooms on the second floor shared a bathroom but the master bedroom had its very own en-suite. Michelle pushed open the door to the master room and gasped; while its décor and facilities were not too dissimilar to the other rooms this one had the most beautiful balcony outside of it. The girls opened the double doors and stepped outside; wooden chairs were placed on there and taking a seat, they saw the twinkling lights of the town and the darkening mountain on the horizon.

Probably shouldn't look at that for too long, Eimear reminded herself.

Exploring of the chalet completed, Ian had taken them back outside to see the boot room which was nestled in between the chalet they were currently staying in and one of the company's other chalets. This was an area, not too dissimilar from a garage, for the guests to store their snowboards, skis, poles and boots. The boot room was to be shared by both chalets and the same applied for the company's other two chalets on the opposite side of town. On learning that Eimear and Michelle would be working in the chalet next to Emma's and Mark's, the two couples grinned at each other.

While the team had explored, Lucy had cooked a mouth-watering meal for them and when it was ready, they all sat down together at the wooden oak table to eat dinner. Eimear, who had initially become possessed by The Fear after seeing the slopes, found her condition only deteriorated once she sampled Ian's and Lucy's high-quality cooking.

There was only one thing for it; if she wanted to overcome The Fear, she was going to have to get absolutely and undeniably inebriated.

CHAPTER 6

The first night in the chalet rapidly declined into a raucous affair. Eimear was no stranger to drink. Christmas parties had always been an excuse for the whole family to get together and have a tipple or two. However, the suggested tipple predictably escalated into a drunken occasion which would end in the early hours of the morning with Uncle Declan puking in the garden and the aunties prancing around the Christmas tree, butchering the vocals of Wham or Live Aid at the top of their voices into a 'microphone' (often the poker from the fire and other utensils from the kitchen).

For years, Eimear, her brothers and her cousins had watched this behaviour in innocent bewilderment, not quite understanding how 'fruit juices' could make the adults behave in such a way. Their initial confusion would quickly pass as they forgot about the adults' odd behaviour and returned to playing games in the bedroom of whichever cousin's house the party was taking place in. But one by one, they started to enter the curious teen years and it wasn't long before they had started sneaking drink from the drinks cabinets for their own experimentation. In their ignorance, they would pour spirits, beers and wine into a large bowl with any mixer they could find, thinking that was how it was done. They would then take it in turns to drink the potent concoction, hiding their repulsion, thinking they were supposed to like it. Then, one after another, they would be sick into the toilet bowl, all while hiding it from the adults who, unbeknownst to them, were already in their own world of intoxication and completely oblivious to their children's behaviour. Each year, the cousins would swear they would never touch a drop again. But as the years wore on, each one turned a little bit older and therefore, alcohol-wiser. Each Christmas, they would bring their newly acquired knowledge to the Christmas party and make a slightly less repulsive mix for their cousins to drink. Eimear learnt a lot from her older brothers and cousins and as she progressed through senior school, she was the one at her friends' house parties who was called upon to make cocktails which would lead to hilarious behaviour and stories for years to come.

It was this same knowledge that she was going to depend upon tonight to ease her nerves.

Although she admitted getting intoxicated on the first night would not give her new employers a good impression of her, she had a plan. She would take the rest of the team down with her. Luckily, she was not the only one who believed drink was an effective medicinal remedy for nerves and found everyone else quite willing to be taken down the path of inappropriate and irresponsible alcohol consumption. After Ian and Lucy had bid the team farewell and had scampered off to their own luxury chalet down the road, Eimear had started making various concoctions and it wasn't long before the team had the partying bug.

"I feel it is necessary," Eimear announced, somewhat incoherently, "that we all get to know each other better. I feel the appropriate place for this to happen is in a pub. Let us go and explore the town and find a drinking hole which will allow such familiarities to take place."

And so they all agreed, town would be their next stop. Eimear, who was convinced that she did not need to wrap up in her layers as "alcohol jackets are so effective these days", had to be manhandled like a child into her ski gear by Michelle who, for all of her drunkenness, did not deteriorate into an imbecile like her friend.

At St. Mary's, the girls had been taught that in the story of creation, on the sixth day, God made man. What they weren't told was that God must have been having an off day when he decided where on his planet to place his new-found creation. Picture him, sitting up on his pearly white throne in the sky amongst the clouds with a two-dimensional map of the world, (which looks fairly similar to a Risk game board), placing little plastic figures, each one representing one of his new creation, at various intervals across the board. Maybe he was so looking forward to the seventh day, his day of rest, that he thought his new creation would be quite happy in L'Homme, a small town in that new mountain range area he had created, for a few days and never considered moving them after his well-earned relax time. Maybe he just didn't care who was placed where. Whatever his reason, his oversight led to L'Homme being dominated by the male species at a ratio of five men to one woman. If the men were all carbon copies of the beautiful, testosterone-filled, muscular, sensitive gentleman who monopolised Eimear's fantasies (who quite often featured the washboard stomach of the Spartan soldiers in 300), this town would be a godsend to all women. However, the reality was somewhat different.

In L'Homme (or L'Whore as it was often called by those who lived there for the season), watching men hunt for women was like watching the mating season of lions on the Discovery Channel. While the team wandered through the snowy streets in search of a bar, a pack of male ski bums sat in their usual watering hole, each clutching a pint and sizing one another up to see whose turn it would be to take on the dominant role of pack leader. As they each chugged on their drinks to see who could down the most as a test of masculinity, the door of the bar opened and Eimear walked through. The heads of the pack suddenly stirred as they caught the hint of female pheromones in the air. They sniffed and looked around to discover the source of this new scent. Necks craned towards the front of the bar and there she was, a real life woman!

"First round on me!" the poor unsuspecting girl cried to her friends and made her way to the bar. Slowly, one by one, each of the men stood and surreptitiously moved together as a unit, as though a lion creeping towards their unsuspecting sexual prey. They circled her, clenching a butt cheek here or flexing an arm muscle there, maybe throwing in a cheeky smile for luck. Each man performed this sexual routine in the hope that she would be impressed with one of their displays of masculine physique and choose them to be her lucky man for the night. Eimear had not been aware that she had been sending out any 'pick up' signals but was instantly flattered by all of the attention. What she did not realise was that it was not ever necessary to send out a signal to warrant such attention. These men did not work to such social norms; a woman could have the biggest wedding ring on her finger and her husband perched on her arm but still, she would be victim to the sexual performance of the pack. As long as there were two breasts (any size), over the age of consent (did not matter how far over) and a pulse (does not necessarily have to be a strong one), the men would be there, preening themselves in front of the female species, desperation emitting from every pore in the hope that tonight might be the night when they finally 'got some'.

Eimear, still not realising that she was not getting the attention for any special reason other than she was female, leant back against the bar in an attempt to look sultry and observed the group of guys who stood on show before her. Her disappointment was instantaneous; not a washboard stomach or attractive face between them. They all looked as though their wardrobe was modelled on that of Kevin from the film Kevin and Perry Go Large. Each man before her came equipped with Kevin's famous long curtains, goofy smile, backwards cap (or, as is more common in a ski resort, a ridiculously long, baggy hat that covers half of one's eyes), the unnecessarily large, extremely baggy clothes and, most importantly, his desperation for sex in order to 'pop his [ski season] cherry'. Not quite the exotic Spartan soldier Eimear was hoping for.

One of the Kevin lookalikes leaned in towards her. "Hi, my name is Bob. I have a penis, you have a vagina. Let's mate."

Eimear was aghast, but then assumed that she must have misheard it thanks to her level of inebriation. Surely no one would actually use that as a chat up line?

She asked the man before her to repeat himself.

"I said, I have a penis, you have a vagina. Let's mate."

She apparently wasn't inebriated enough. Mortification flooded through every inch of her body. Surely this was a joke? He could not actually think that line would get him somewhere? Her eyes darted to the rest of the group to see if a twinkle in someone's eye or maybe a cheeky grin would reveal that it was in fact a joke, or even, please God, a dare. She hoped beyond hope that one of the other guys would slap this Bob on the back, mock him for using such a crap pick up line, then turn towards her, tell her she had beautiful eyes and salvage the situation. But there were no such signs or such luck.

What she didn't realise was that as the Bobs (as she decided to brand them) travel in packs with like-minded people, they shared the same ideas. They talked to each other, swapped notes and tips on how to 'catch' women, each believing that lines like that were completely acceptable. Even worse, each and every one of them believed themselves to be modern day Casanovas.

As the silence lengthened, the severity of the situation dawned on Eimear; these clueless guys had actually used that as a genuine chat up line and so expected a serious response. She closed her eyes, breathed in deeply for ten seconds and then uttered a silent prayer to the Saint of unsuspecting victims at the thought of the poor virtuous girls in the future who would also be on the receiving end of that line.

Even with all of her naivety, Eimear still knew how a guy should speak to a girl if he wanted a chance with her. This was certainly not it; for the sake of women everywhere, she had to end this now and educate them. The best way to do this was obviously to snort. And then laugh in their faces.

As she clutched her sides laughing hysterically, her reaction was met by confused silence. The Bobs looked at one another in bewilderment, as though to question why it was not working this time as it had always had a 100% success rate whenever executed. Seeing this reaction made her howl harder.

Seeing that she was getting nowhere, Eimear, who had alcohol-fuelled courage, decided to go for the direct approach.

"Shite line guys, it is not going to get you anywhere. I bid you farewell."

With that, feeling slightly smug at how bad ass and nonchalant she sounded, she picked up the tray with all the drinks for her table on it and wandered back to her new friends. But something was not right; she had the distinct feeling that she was not alone. Glancing over her shoulder, she noticed she was being followed. All of the Bobs were chasing after her in single file, one hand clasping a pint, the other grabbing their over-sized belts in an attempt to pull up their sagging trousers.

I am the pied bloody piper of L'Homme, she thought to herself. Oh well, might as well let them join us, they aren't causing any real harm.

But Eimear had just made a critical mistake. By not shooing them away instantly, she had only encouraged them. She should have realised the moment Bob (number 1) opened his mouth and uttered that fateful line that this could not end well. She should have read the signs and instantly taken out a restraining order on each and every one of them. But damn that kind and naïve nature of hers! She was now a marked woman.

She approached the table monopolised by her new friends and the Bobs' faces lit up; there was more than one girl there. Result! Before Eimear even had a chance to explain that these guys had followed her and she could only assume that they wanted to join them, the Bobs descended on the table, nestling in amongst all of the team. It did not matter that the other six out of the seven people already sitting there were in a relationship. It did not matter that the members of each couple were sitting side by side. The Bobs burrowed their way in amongst the girls and attempted to work their flawed charm on all of them.

Seeing the destruction that was being caused, Eimear immediately returned to the bar and ordered a bucket full of Sambuca shots for her team.

They were going to need them.

CHAPTER 7

Eimear stirred. As she started to wake, she moved her head slightly and realised that her face was balancing on the verge of an uncomfortable precipice. She sleepily shifted the rest of her body ever so slightly and discovered that she had extremely numb bum cheeks, most likely caused from sitting on a strange, cold, hard surface. Her body also appeared to be covered in goose pimples. God she was cold. And then she realised.

She was completely naked.

She slowly opened one of her eyes and looked at her surroundings.

Oh God.

She squeezed it shut, counted to five and slowly opened both of her eyes together.

It was as she feared. She had done it after all, on her first night too. For the love of God, did she have no sense or pride?

There comes a time in every girl's life when she realises that her mother might just have been right about quite a lot of things. When things get really bad, there comes a time in every girl's life when she knows it. When alcohol is involved, there is a time in every Catholic girl's life when they wish they had taken advice from not only their mother but the Church too.

When things really hit rock bottom, an individual realises all of these things at the same time.

Today was that day.

On her first night in a new job in a strange country surrounded by people she didn't know but needed to impress, she had fallen asleep with her head inside the toilet bowl.

Her mother's anxious warning reverberated in her mind.

"You are too small to drink! People as tiny as you think they can hack it, decide to have a drink, get the hangover from hell the next day and eventually die from liver disease!"

Well the first bit was certainly true but she had a few years to wait to discover if the second premonition materialised. God, she hated it when her mother was right!

33

She slowly peeled her cheek away from the toilet seat, lifted her head out of the toilet bowl, raised her hand to the toilet handle and flushed her sick away. She licked her dry mouth, rested her head against her hand and when the spinning subsided slightly, crawled along the cold bathroom tiles towards the towel rail. Draping a bath towel over her back to cover her nudity, she slithered along the floor, through the bathroom door, along the tiny corridor and into her bedroom.

Thank God she and Michelle had been given the downstairs bedroom and no one had yet materialised, she thought, as she slowly lifted herself into her bed. As she lay back amongst the covers, panting slightly from the effort, she surveyed the chaos scattered around her temporary bedroom. Her clothes from the night before were thrown on the floor in a line leading to the bathroom, as though she was Gretel leaving a reminder of how to return to the bed with her trail of bread crumbs.

Why do I always have to get naked whenever I am sick? She berated herself.

In a single bed on the opposite side of the room, an unconscious lump snored beneath a mound of bed clothes, an indication of Michelle's presence. Propped up against their bedroom door was a ten-foot-long flag pole, equipped with a limp flag advertising the logo from one of the many local ski schools. She stared at it aghast; how in the name of sweet Jesus had they managed to get that into their room? Where had it come from? And more importantly, how in the name of good God were they going to get it out?

Her head throbbed and stomach lurched and for some bizarre reason, her mind was cast back to her Confirmation day. At the age of 11, all of the girls in Eimear's year were expected to participate in this sacrament and asked whether they still wanted to be part of the Church.

Each child was allowed to choose the name of a saint to whom they would look for moral guidance for the rest of their lives. If they gave the correct answer (which was, of course, a resounding 'yes'), their belief was blessed and they were confirmed under their new saint name, symbolising their admittance as full members into the Catholic Church. Of course, saying no was not an option.

She made two significant mistakes that day. The first was her confirmation name. Barbara. Saint bloody Barbara. On reflection, Eimear was convinced that she was a victim of child abuse as her parents did not intervene and prevent her from choosing that appalling, stuffy, old name.

The second was not agreeing to be a teetotaller, a lifestyle they had to decide as part of the service. She blamed her father for this.

She remembered approaching the alter, walking up the steps towards some high priest with a funny hat on and kneeling before him. She was then asked by Father Joseph, who stood beside him, whether she would be agreeing to a life free from the sin of alcohol or not. She had given the question a lot of thought and had discussed it extensively with her parents. Her mother had been all for it.

"Just think of your poor liver!"

Her father had been against it.

"Listen love," he had said, patting her on the back. "Whilst I am obviously very concerned for your liver, there are reasons why people drink and I feel it is my responsibility to inform you of the pros whilst your mother fills you in on the cons so you can make an informed decision. People drink to have fun, at parties for example, or on your birthday and even your wedding night. These are all occasions which benefit from drinking a few."

When she had queried why her wedding night would require her to drink, her dad had turned red, used the age-old line "You'll understand when you are older" and then had run into a different room away from the piercing, accusatory eyes of her mother.

Eimear remembered the look of disappointment etched across her priest's face when she had informed him she would not live a life without drink and she cursed herself bitterly. Why did she have to be such a bad Catholic, run away to France in a guilt-free quest for boys and get blind drunk in the process?

Oh God. Boys.

She clutched the pint of water someone had the sense to place, somewhat precariously, in the corner of her bed and downed half of the contents quickly in an attempt to block out the events from the previous night which had just come rushing back to her. Oh how she wished she was still unconscious with her head down the toilet, hair floating in the fetid water amongst the chunks of sick.

Images flashed through her mind; Sambuca shots, Jagerbombs, the boys in her team telling the Bobs to 'do one' and leave their girlfriends alone, the Bobs deciding to give up with the other girls and targeting only her and Michelle; more drink to deal with the unwanted attention; someone suggesting a club; there was a cage in this club; Eimear dancing in the cage; a Bob climbing into the cage, taking a particular shine to her and trying to put his arm around her; running away from this Bob and hiding in the toilets for a while; emerging from the toilets after what was deemed to be a safe hiding time; another Bob approaching her and shaking some bizarre moves in her direction; a hip shimmy here, a crotch lunge there, a swirl or two... then a dive for her mouth; Eimear shrugging her shoulders in a gesture to show compliance; Eimear being sick in this Bob's mouth as his washing-machine tongue devoured her face, allowing dollops of drool to leak into her mouth; being sick in the club toilets; the lights being switched on and being told they had to leave; a stalker.

Eimear's memory did a double take; a stalker?

Oh yes, the stalker. Now she remembered it vividly.

The lights rose in the club and the happy inebriated team staggered outside into their new snowy world, singing raucously at the top of their voices. As they made their way home, stopping at various intervals to skate on the ice rink, throw snow balls at one another and apparently steal giant flag poles, Eimear became aware of an alien presence amongst the group. Washing-machine-tongue Bob was following them home. What Eimear still did not realise was that nothing will ever deter a Bob once they have marked their prey. By allowing him to violate her mouth, she had given him the impression she was keen. It did not matter that his desire was not reciprocated, nor that she had puked into his mouth. He had caught a girl and nothing was going to stop him from trying to get his end wet. Eimear, annoyed that her ice-skating moves were being interrupted by this lech, decided to get rid of him once and for all. She had tried everything from asking him somewhat politely to 'piss right off' to getting all of the guys to tell him not so politely that if he took another step in their direction, they would 'thump him'. Even the threat of violence did not deter him, but merely caused him to follow them at a distance, ducking behind an inanimate object whenever one of them glanced in his direction. In the end, drastic measures were taken; while the girls bundled into a doorway and formed a protective circle around Eimear, the guys lined the edge of the doorway and pretended to relieve themselves. The girls spied on washing-machine-tongue Bob from their safe hiding place; it was as though they were watching a monkey who had just lost the fruit he had picked. He stopped in the middle of the street and raised his arms so they were level to his chest and made a gesture that conveyed his confusion. 'How have I lost her? I was stalking her so well!' it said. He slowly rotated 360 degrees looking up and down the street as he did and then, admitting defeat, shrugged and wandered back into town, probably to choose another innocent target to follow home.

She shuddered as she remembered the deposits of saliva that washing-machine-tongue Bob had left in her mouth, retched and gulped the remains of the water in an attempt to remove any trace.

There was a knock at the door. Eimear, with all of the energy she could muster, covered herself with her blanket and pathetically called out 'come in'. Leanne, the 30-year-old dentist, stuck her head around the door.

"Good morning drunkards." Michelle started stirring beneath the mound and grunted in recognition.

"Andrew and I are cooking a feast fit for kings, or at least for the extremely hungover. How about you shower then come into the kitchen and get some food inside you? Training starts in an hour and I have a feeling Lucy and Ian will not have much patience for our current states."

The door shut and Michelle sat up in bed, clutching her head.

"Never again," she moaned and staggered off towards the bathroom.

At the sound of the shower being switched on, Eimear leant back against her cushions to savour the last few moments of peace before she was expected to face the day. Her phone beeped; annoyed at having to move from her comfortable spot, she reached over to her bedside cabinet and grabbed it. Expecting to see a message from her mum, she half-heartedly opened the text message. It was from an unknown number:

Great to meet you last night,

shame we got separated on the way home.

Hope to see you around soon. X

Washing-machine-tongue Bob had her French number, something she had courtesy of her family who had bought her an old-school Nokia from French Amazon as a leaving present. Her regret for sharing her number grew at the same rate as her nausea and she slumped beneath her quilt in an attempt to hide away from the world. Today was going to be a very long day.

CHAPTER 8

Eimear gripped the steering wheel of the van and breathed in through her nose for a few seconds, held it, then slowly released her breath out through her mouth. When she had quelled her nerves, she turned the key in the ignition, placed her foot on the clutch, pushed it as far down to the ground as possible and tried to move the gear stick from neutral into first. Except that she could not quite reach the floor of the van. She pulled the seat a few inches further towards the steering wheel, shuffled to the edge of the driver's seat and tried again. Still too far away from the pedal. Frustrated with the shortness of her legs, she banged her fists against the wheel, then rested her head on her stilled hands.

She was fed up; this was not how she had envisaged the start of her ski season. She had spent the week up to her elbows in cobwebs, dirty laundry and cleaning equipment. She was covered in dust, her eyes were red from inadvertently spraying Cif into them and she had consumed half a bar of diluted soap which she had accidentally knocked into her cup of tea whilst she scrubbed a filthy bath tap, only to realise as she neared the bottom of the cup and a few undiluted fragments loomed before her eyes. Having never been an overly tidy person, cleaning four chalets, let alone four chalets in under a week, was her version of hell and Ian and Lucy, she had decided, were the devils. After discovering a hungover team and a ten-foot flag pole in the girls' room, they had been, as Leanne had correctly guessed, quite unimpressed by their behaviour and had put the team through their paces. To make matters worse, when they had eventually moved into their unsophisticated staff accommodation, ironically named 'The Palace', there had been no hot water or heating as the fuse box had blown. Eimear and Michelle, who were sharing a room, had spooned one another in the bottom bed of their bunk for a little heat, whilst dressed in as many layers of their warmest ski gear as possible.

Life, she had thought whilst shivering in the arms of her friend, could not get much worse. That was until she had been sent out on her own in one of the company vans to get some more cleaning supplies for the chalet.

Driving in the snow meant learning about the use and importance of snow chains. Ideally a lesson could have been given outside in the snow with a vehicle at hand, but Ian and Lucy preferred not to stand in the snow, as it was a bit cold. So, while Eimear and Michelle were cleaning the fourth and final chalet, the one which had been their luxury home for the first few days, the voice of Lucy summoned them to the living room.

Walking into the room, the first thing they saw was a large old tyre on the table Ruth had so thoroughly cleaned only hours before. Lying next to the dirty tyre was a rusty set of snow chains which looked like an instrument of medieval torture or, for want of a better comparison, a DNA double helix.

Ignoring the sceptical looks of their team, Ian and Lucy proceeded to demonstrate how to tie the chains onto the tyre, manoeuvring the wheel with ease as they did so. Everyone was invited to have a go and, when it was Eimear's turn, she had managed to weave the chains easily around the back and over the top of the tyre, tying them tightly at the front as they had been shown.

She was surprised at how simple the process had been but then, she had been able to adjust the angle of the tyre and pick it up when she needed to cover the bottom of it with chains. She suspected that handling a wheel underneath a beast of a van and covered in an inch of snow might be a rather different proposition.

Now sitting unsupervised in the driver's seat, she ran over the important points they had been taught only a few days before in case she encountered really thick or icy snow on the way to the shops on her mission to buy more Cif and cloths. Number one, do not use them on the road unless it is completely covered in a foot of snow.

Number two, only use them if the van gets stuck in snow or if you do not think you will be able to climb up a steep incline. She peered through the windscreen at the clear blue sky. Please oh please do not start snowing on the way to the shops, she begged the sky. I do not think I will be able to hack it!

With a deep breath and a fresh wave of determination, she tugged at the seat one more time, pulled it in as far as it could possibly go, strained her leg and finally, pushed the clutch all the way down to the ground. With a little yelp of success, she shoved the gear into first, lifted her foot ever so slightly off the clutch, pressed the accelerator and felt the van move forward. She was driving a van! She was really doing it!

And then she stalled.

She was not a great driver at the best of times, let alone when she was driving a two-tonne van. There had been the odd incident or two at home which had made her parents question whether she had in fact genuinely passed her driving test, or if she had somehow bribed the examiner. A police officer had pulled her over for not leaving enough space between her and the car in front when changing lanes, an action, he claimed, which had nearly killed her. Then there was the time she had misjudged the amount of space there was in her drive and had somehow reversed her dear old faithful Toyota Corolla onto the driveway wall. When she had eventually managed to remove the side of her car and the majority of the silver paint work from the bricks with the help of her brothers, she had spent an hour trying to convince her parents that the scratches along the length of the car had been there when they had bought it and the flecks of silver paint on the wall must have been an act of vandalism from the local thugs. Needless to say, her argument failed her terribly and she was banned from driving for a month afterwards. When she was allowed to drive again, she drove the wrong way up a one-way street and nearly killed a cyclist, all because she had been distracted by singing along to the radio, using her fist as a microphone. When her parents found out that little gem, they had taken her car keys off her and said she should not expect to get her car back until the day she was wed. Eimear thought she would never drive again. She had kept these little details to herself when she had been interviewed, claiming she was a fantastic driver and had lots of experience. She was convinced she would be fine, how hard could it be? But she had failed to remember that the van was going to be a lot bigger than her faithful Toyota Corolla, the loveable little car she had abandoned in lieu of her new life abroad.

She took another deep breath, turned the van on a second time and repeated the process.

I just need to get used to the size and remember to drive on the right, she told herself, as the van started to creep forward.

She left the drive, went to the correct side of the road and slowly started increasing her speed. The roads were clear of snow, fresh snowplough tracks revealing that they had been out earlier that morning clearing the roads for all of the traffic. Her confidence grew as she covered more distance and she started to believe that this would be easier than she had expected. She hummed to herself and switched a local radio station on for a bit of company; a song which reminded her of nights out at home came on and soon, she was belting along at the top of her voice. Her body started swaying from side to side as she sung, her mood getting better by the second; that was until she spotted a roundabout in the distance.

"Oh dear," she whispered.

Panicking, she tried to remember which direction she would normally enter a roundabout when at home so that she could do the opposite in France. In her terror, her mind went blank; "Come on, come on!" she said out loud to the empty bus. But no divine inspiration or sign appeared, telling her what to do. She hoped there would be another car on the roundabout so that she could copy them but, as she drove closer, she had no such luck. She stopped the van just before she entered the roundabout and studied the traffic island before her, looking to her left and right as she did. And then she had a brilliant idea.

If a tree falls and there is no one there to hear it, does it really make a sound? she thought to herself. So, if I go the wrong way around the roundabout and there is no one to see it, did I really make a mistake?

She was not a gambling girl but she was willing to be a little bit daring and take a chance on this occasion. She could see the shops a little bit further down the road to the left of the round-about. With a glance in all of her mirrors and out of her windows to ensure no other cars were coming, she indicated and, using the left-hand side of the lane, drove on to the roundabout, then exited at the first opportunity. So busy was she congratulating herself on her clever idea, Eimear failed see to the 'A' bus hurtling towards her. The sound of a loud, long horn brought her attention back to the road and she realised was driving on the wrong side of the road!

Eimear was no normal, rational person and with the huge bus heading directly for her, confidence, reason and all spatial-awareness fled, leaving her with nothing but clumsiness and panic for a friend. Instead of just calmly moving over to the other lane, she aggressively jerked the steering wheel, swerving the van across to the other side of the road.

And as the bus hurtled passed her, the driver gesticulating angrily through the window, she heard a bang.

She stomped on the breaks, panic spreading through her body.

"Sweet Jesus," she whispered into the silence. "I've killed someone."

Her knuckles turned white as she clutched the steering wheel with all of the strength she could muster. She couldn't move; the thought of stepping out of the van and seeing the cold, stiff body of the poor unsuspecting victim she had just removed from this mortal world chilled her to the bone. Her parents were going to kill her. She could kiss her place at University College Dublin, the university she would be attending the following September, goodbye. Instead, she would spend the next twenty years in a French jail learning French by candle light.

A knock at the driver's window made her jump. She turned her head, half expecting to see a policeman waiting for her, his chiselled features illuminated by the flashing blue and white lights from his car. In the distance, a forensic team would be examining the body which would be strewn across the snowy ground.

She really needed to stop watching CSI.

The reality was somewhat different. Waiting for her was not, as she had expected, a handcuff-waving member of the

Gendarmerie nationale, but an exceptionally angry twenty-something-year-old waving a smashed, detached wing mirror in one hand, a clenched fist with the other.

A beautiful twenty-something-year-old, she noticed, one with the most mesmerising deep blue eyes she had ever seen in her life.

A pure Adonis stood before her. The man at her window was tall, had broad shoulders, and through his tight-fitted ski jacket, she could tell he had a well-toned physique. Thinking about what might be beneath his jacket was enough to make her go a bit dizzy.

His hatless head revealed he had brown, wavy, short hair which was combed in a side parting, creating a nice tousled effect. She really wanted to run her fingers through it.

Along his jaw line was one-day-old stubble, the kind which looked as though it had been groomed with a purpose and not some pre-pubescent runt's attempt to grow the smallest bit of bum fluff.

His upper torso was all that was visible through the window but she strained forward slightly to see if she could see more.

However, she quickly sat back when she caught sight of his beautiful face which was contorted in anger and shouting rather abusive obscenities at her in what she rather excitedly recognised to be a strong Dublin accent.

"Oi!" The angry man knocked again. "Are you getting out or what?"

Eimear cautiously wound down her window, not willing to leave the van unless it was absolutely necessary to do so. Although he was beautiful, he was angry and she didn't want to get too close… yet. When the window could be lowered no further, she tried to look over the angry man's shoulder to try and see if there was in fact a body.

"Um… excuse me?" Angry Man was off again, "May I have your attention please? Did you not see my van parked on the side of the road? Any reason why you decided to plough into my wing mirror and completely remove it?"

Reality slowly dawned on Eimear. Trying to suppress her

excited smile she stuttered, "You mean…. I haven't killed any-one? There isn't a body? I don't have to flee the country? I just hit your wing mirror?"

Confusion filled angry man's face.

"Er… what? Are you ok?" he questioned suspiciously. "Are you on drugs? Should you even be driving?" He started looking at her like she was possibly a little bit crazy. "You thought you had killed someone? Is there an ounce of logic in that head of yours?"

"Not really, no. To all of the above." Eimear responded, shrug-ging as she did. "Except yes to me thinking I had killed some-one."

Angry Man sighed, rolled his eyes and said in a tired, resigned voice, "Right well, I am going to have to get your name, number and insurance details so that I can get this mess fixed and sort it out with your insurance company."

A new fear flooded Eimear. To find out the insurance details, she would have to call Lucy and Ian. To call Lucy and Ian would be admitting she had done something wrong, so soon after the incident with the melted blender; how was she supposed to know plastic melted in the dishwasher? Discovering she had van-dalised someone else's van would push them over the edge and she would never hear the end of it. My God, she suddenly thought, maybe they would even send me home?

Eimear tried to suppress her panic. Maybe she could salvage the situation and keep the terrible two from discovering her destructive secret.

"Um… I'm sorry, I don't know your name?" she asked, attempting what she hoped was a friendly and not creepy smile as she did.

"Ryan."

"Right, Ryan. I'm Eimear, I am from Cork. It is very nice to meet you."

Her attempt at formalities was met with an icy, dubious stare.

"Well… um…" she continued after the pregnant pause, "look Ryan. My bosses are a particular breed of knobby and are not my biggest fans. Hearing about something like this would really not

45

make my life worth living. Can I do a deal with you?"

Her question was once again met with silence.

Jesus, Eimear thought, he is really not making this easy for me.

She cleared her throat. God almighty, it was dry.

"Well, how about I just fix it for you? I don't mean personally, obviously. Haha! I mean, come on, these guns couldn't even build a Lego van, let alone fix a real one." She let out another nervous laugh as she tensed her pathetic excuse for arm muscles, invisible beneath her ski jacket.

Again, her lame attempt at a joke was met with the icy glare and further silence.

Tough crowd, she thought, before carrying on.

"What I mean is, if you get it fixed and give me the receipt, I will pay whatever it costs. I will give you my name, phone number, place of work and most importantly, my word that I will follow through on this promise. You can even test the number before we part to make sure I have given you the real one."

She waited with bated breath for his response, her heart beating against her chest with an unrecognisable force.

My God, he really does have beautiful eyes, she thought, as she stared hopefully into them. He certainly was very fit. She started nibbling her lip and, without noticing, twirling her hair around her finger as she cocked her head slightly towards him.

Eventually, after what felt like a life time, Ryan cracked a small smile. "OK," he agreed, much to Eimear's relief, "but you need to drive more carefully from now on. It is only a van you are driving, not a tank of mass destruction, although with you behind the wheel, who knows."

Relief flooded through Eimear; she detached her fingers from her now completely tangled hair with some difficulty and searched through the glove box. She found a pen and piece of paper, scribbled down the relevant details and after he had checked her phone number, she started apologising profusely for her mistake.

"Don't worry about it, I'll be in touch. Speak to you soon, Accidental Eimear." And with that, Ryan sloped off towards his own, newly deformed van.

After she had saved his number from his missed call on her phone (Blue-eyed Ryan!), she continued driving towards the shops to complete her cleaning product mission. She was haunted by those piercing blue eyes. Although she had meant to drive with newly found caution, without realising it, she had taken one hand off the steering wheel whilst twirling her hair around her fingers again. She found herself hoping that, once the wing mirror mess was rectified, she would see those mesmeric, piercing, blue eyes around the town.

The sound of her phone beeping brought her back to her senses. A teeny firework exploded in her stomach.

To her slight embarrassment, she hoped it would be from him.

Eager to read the text, she arrived in the supermarket carpark and swerved into the closest available parking space, completely unaware that she was taking up two parking spaces. She turned off the engine and started scrambling through her bag, her impatience at discovering the sender of the text impeding her search somewhat. When she finally found her phone caught up amongst a pair of ski socks and some cleaning rags, she opened up the text message.

Her disappointment was instantaneous.

It was Washing-Machine-Tongue Bob again, never to be deterred even though his previous message had been ignored.

Haven't seen you out over the last few nights,
fancy meeting up for a drink later?
My treat. X

Eimear hesitated, threw her phone onto the passenger seat, thought for a moment, picked it up again and re-read the message. Every nerve in her body screamed at her to delete the text, place her phone back in her bag and get on with her Cif mission. But something stopped her; maybe it was her fear that, if she had many more run-ins like that on the road, she would be returning to Ireland in a coffin and so only had a limited time to meet guys. Maybe it was because the thought of the blue-eyed Adonis ever being interested in her seemed too far-fetched so she might as well accept a drink from the one and only person who had shown any interest in her since she arrived. Maybe it was because she had had such a crap week and had been going to bed early since that fateful first night, she needed an excuse to go out and have some fun. Part of her too suspected that she had imagined the extremity of how bad that night had been and, if she met Washing-Machine-Tongue Bob sober, might see a decent, non-sloppy side to him. Whatever it was, she found her fingers replying:

Sounds good, 9 o'clock at The Cow Bell? X

With that, she hopped out of the van, locked the doors and wandered inside the shop to search for the Cif. Maybe her season would not be so bad after all.

CHAPTER 9

Eimear pushed open the front door of the bar, scuttled inside quickly to get out of the cold and looked around. She had not paid much attention to the décor of the bar on her first night, but now she gazed at the place in admiration. It was beautiful; dark wooden booths with old oak tables lined one of the long walls whilst empty barrels surrounded with stools were used as tables in the middle of the floor. The bar itself lined the opposite wall but instead of the stereotypical wood used elsewhere in the bar, the top of it was covered with slate, a reminder of the old industry which used to exist in the town before it became a ski attraction town for tourists. Old cart wheels, ski poles and various types of skis, all extremely aged, were randomly hung around the bar while both antique and modern pictures of the surrounding mountains, both in the summer and winter, were scattered in between. Cattle and farmers watched the drinkers from various pieces of art, and a cow bell, which had been hung above the doorway, clanged constantly, signifying the arrival or departure of customers. Further bells were scattered around the room, both on the ceiling and the walls and if someone tipped the bar staff, a cow bell was rung as a reminder to other customers to dig deep. L'Homme, as well as making money from tourism, was also a dairy town and was famous for its cheeses, some of which were sold all around the world. The tolling bells were a reminder to each person to be proud or impressed by the town's heritage.

After taking in the marvellous décor, she decided to wander deeper into the bar in search of Washing-Machine and as she did so, a terrible realisation descended upon her. She could not really remember what Washing-Machine looked like, or his real name. If her drunken memory served her well, she remembered vaguely that he had brown hair which reached just below his chin, stubble and wore baggy clothing, but then who didn't around here? How the hell would she differentiate him from the numerous other saggy baggy elephants, or address him?

She hoped that, once she spotted him, her memory would kick

in. Whilst she searched the bar for her distraction from cleaning, Michelle's lecture resonated in her mind.

"You ran away from him for a reason, don't come crying to me when you have turned deaf from your ears being filled with his dribble and don't you dare get drunk, you have your first ski lesson tomorrow. If you are not home by 11, I am going to come looking for you. Don't you roll your eyes at me young lady, I know what you are like! The concept of one drink simply does not exist in your mind!"

Oh blah, blah and blah, Eimear thought to herself, she is not my bloody mother. But oh God, my first ski lesson!

Her stomach immediately contracted into one undoable knot at the thought. She glanced over at the bar.

One drink is all I need, she thought, then that will put skiing out of my mind and give me the tiny confidence boost I need to speak to Washing-Machine. She leaned over the bar, caught the attention of the bartender and ordered a glass of wine, the size of which quickly changed from a small to a large on hearing the price only differed by a euro. As she was waiting for her change, someone tapped her on her shoulder and whispered in her ear, "How would you like me to make your breakfast for you in the morning?"

She looked the guy who had uttered the pitiful line up and down; a man roughly forty years her superior stood before her in the baggiest clothing she had seen yet. He winked at her, slurped on his pint and then said, "well?"

You would think he would know better. She didn't even bother responding, just rolled her eyes, shot him a wilting look, grabbed her wine from the bar and walked towards a guy she had just noticed sitting by himself in one of the booths in the furthest corner of the bar. He looked vaguely familiar and he had all the makings of Washing-Machine. Feeling slightly confident and impressed with her ability to find him so easily, she wandered over to him. He was playing on his phone and did not notice her approaching until she was standing right beside him.

"Hiya!" she said, a little too loudly for her liking, and gave a wave of her hand. Aware that she was still waving, she quickly hid her hand behind her back and waited for his look of recognition. It didn't come.

"Um... hi?" he responded.

"Do you mind?" she asked, gesturing at the empty chair opposite him and, without waiting for an answer, sat down. She pushed the empty wine glass that had been occupying the table in front of her to the side and replaced it with her own full one.

"God, I am glad I found you, I didn't think I would be able to remember what you looked like. But here you are! So how have you been?"

"Um... fine... thanks. You?"

"Yeah, yeah good. Sorry, hang on, can I help you?"

She had turned to address an older woman who had materialised by the table and appeared to be glaring at her.

"Yes, yes you can. You are sitting in my seat and talking to my boyfriend."

Eimear looked around at the neighbouring tables and then looked back at the angry woman.

"Sorry, I am talking to your whom?"

"My boyfriend!" she exclaimed, gesturing at – apparently not – Washing-Machine-Tongue Bob.

Oh shit, Eimear thought to herself as she realised what she had done. She jumped up, knocking the table as she did so, sloshing beer and wine all over the table and smashing the empty wine glass. Eimear started uttering apology after apology, whilst trying to mop up the beer and wine infusion with her sleeve and collect the shards of glass in her other hand.

"Oh for God's sake!" the woman muttered. "Just move will you," she ordered, as she started cleaning the table with a cloth that had magically appeared in her hand.

Eimear grabbed what was left of her wine and started to back away from the table.

"Look, I am really sorry, just got you confused with someone else. Um... so... are you two doing a season?" Her attempt at making small talk was met with furious eyes.

"No we are not, we are just visiting friends. Not that it is any of your business. Now go away!"

Relieved that she would not have to see those people again, she turned and hurried away to the opposite side of the bar, to be as far away as possible from the raging woman.

Well if that is not him, where is he? She thought to herself as a frantic movement caught her eye.

A young guy who had the face of a baby and shared a close resemblance to Cartman from South Park was sitting at a barrel table and was waving in her direction. She smiled dismissively at him and then continued looking around the bar whilst fishing in her bag for her now ringing mobile. 'Washing-Machine' flashed up on the screen.

"Hello?"

"Over here! You have just seen me!"

Eimear, surprised that she had missed him, turned around and saw the waving guy. Her eyes glanced over him and continued to skirt across the bar.

"Where did you say you were?"

"Right in front of you! I am waving at you!"

Eimear's heart sank; surely not? She hung up the phone and walked up to the waving Cartman. He grinned, stuck out his hand and, on receiving hers, pulled her towards him in a bear-like hug and kissed both of her cheeks. Eimear, still not over the shock of Washing-Machine being Cartman's doppelgänger, did not utter a word.

"You are so funny," he uttered, "pretending not to see me."

Still nothing, not even a squeak emitted from her mouth.

"So..... would you like a drink?" He was looking awkward now and had started to regard her like she was a little bit crazy. Aware that she still had not said anything and was most likely freaking him out, Eimear tried to snap out of her trance.

"Sorry! Sorry. Um, yeah, didn't see you, haha. Um, I am... short-sighted. That's it! I am short-sighted. Can hardly see my own hands in front of my face haha. So, um, yeah...sorry. Drink. Drink! Want me to get you one?"

And without waiting for his answer, she hopped up to the bar and ordered another large glass of wine and a pint for the star of South Park.

A few large gulps of wine later, Eimear who was feeling slightly guilty at her fickleness, felt she might as well make the most
of her evening out. After all, school had always taught them that
one should never judge; reminding herself of this, she thought
that he could be really nice underneath all of that hair (which was
down to his shoulders), facial hair (more like bum fluff, barely
worth growing) and clothing which, she had thought baggy, was
actually just designed to fit his huge body.

"So.... Tell me more about you," she began; she really needed
to find out his real name.

"Well, I am from Birmingham in England, I am sixteen and
moved here straight after school to take up a job as an underwater ceramic technician."

Eimear stared at him. She had kissed a child! He was the same
age as her younger brother! How drunk had she been?

Trying not to show her alarm and slight disgust at her choice
in kissing buddy, she responded, "What is an underwater ceramic technician exactly?"

It sounded pretty impressive, quite an exotic, intelligent job
title actually. Maybe he was some sort of child prodigy,
England's youngest geologist, sent over here to examine the
rocks in the frozen nearby lake. She surreptitiously crossed her
fingers and legs in the hope that it was something exciting and
that the situation still could be remotely salvageable.

"It is a posh way of saying I wash dishes in that big hotel up
the road."

Maybe not. She had heard of the hotel he referred to and was
at least impressed that he had a job there, although somewhat
surprised that the owners had employed this guy before her as it
was an upmarket place to stay, attracting many rich customers.
The hotel was in one of the oldest and most impressive buildings
in the town, made out of original stone and slate from the town's
mines, none of which were in operation any more. It had been
used as the town's hall in the olden days and had even been used
as a jail once. The building had been neglected for a number of
years and was under threat of demolition. The now owners of it
had saved the building from being knocked down and had

restored it to its original beauty. They had then opened it as a hotel and although it only had 10 bedrooms so was small by other hotel standards, it was renowned amongst the locals for being one of the nicest places to not only stay in, but to eat at too. The team had passed a number of times going to and from the chalet and frequently commented on it. Nestling amongst the snow, it looked like a magical place, with a warm, log fire visible and beautifully decorated Christmas tree through the window.

"I see. And your accent?"

"Actually, funny story. I am from Birmingham originally but have a Dudley accent as that is where I grew up. They say it is even worse than the Brummie accent!"

She was never drinking Sambuca again.

In an attempt to buy herself a few extra minutes before she had to say anything, she started slugging on her wine. Cartman, as she was now referring to him in her mind, thought that she was initiating a race. He whooped, picked up his pint and started downing it. Watching him slosh beer down his chin and onto his top, she realised she needed to get out of there. Fast. Excuses started running through her mind; she could fake a heart attack! Too extreme. Maybe she could go to the toilet and crawl out a window. Hmm, too James Bond like and, knowing her, she would get stuck half way through and would be found hours later frozen to death. Oh why oh why didn't she come up with an SOS plan with Michelle before she left! She could have text SAVE ME to her when she went to the toilet and Mitch could have called her with an 'urgent event', thereby giving her a reason to leave; bloody hindsight. Oh but of course, Michelle would not have agreed to participate because she was mad with her for coming. God she hated it when Mitch was right!

Suddenly, Cartman let out a huge burp, patted himself on his chest and then launched into a monologue about his life. More burping followed, more drinks were bought by him for him without Eimear ever being offered one, more self-obsessed conversation and yet again, more burping. Time passed; Eimear sank into a semi-comatose state and tuned out from the verbal diatribe emitting from Cartman's mouth. She didn't even have the heart to go and get herself another drink, but sat on her stool, swirling the last few drops round her wine glass. Suddenly, Cartman stood up and bellowed across the bar,

"Oi! Ryan! Over here mate!"

Eimear froze. It was a fairly common name, she decided, in Ireland anyway and, although L'Homme was small, it would be too coincidental for this oaf (she shot Cartman a dirty look as she thought it) to know the beautiful-eyed man, the one whose van she had massacred only a few hours before. She slowly turned around to see who he was shouting at and, spotting who was coming over to their table, nearly fell off her stool.

Blue-eyed Adonis was in their midst.

Goddammit, she thought. Of all the people Ryan could see her with, it had to be South Park's star.

As she watched Ryan saunter over to their table, she was aware that her mouth was hanging open and there was some saliva hanging off the corner of her mouth. She surreptitiously wiped her lips, then leant her chin on her hand to prevent her mouth from falling open again. Once she felt she had regained some composure and more importantly, control over her body, she resumed ogling at him.

Without the van door in her way, she could now see the rest of Ryan and it was a sight she highly appreciated. Unlike the other men who inhabited the town, he was not wearing overly baggy clothing, did not have a stupid hat on and did not talk like a wannabe gangster. He had tight Levi jeans on and through them, Eimear could see his tight, leg muscles. She found it very diffi-cult to swallow the lump in her throat.

"Hello again Accidental Eimear." Ryan was now smiling at her, anger apparently subsided.

Eimear thought she caught a funny look on his face as he ini-tially saw them together but then assumed she had mistaken it as he smiled at them.

"You two know each other?" Cartman questioned, looking backwards and forwards between them, confusion sketched across his dumb face.

"This lady was the one responsible for the wing mirror."

Cartman let out a huge snort. "That was you?" he guffawed into his pint. "We ripped the piss out of you." More snorting.

Eimear rolled her eyes, her heart sinking at the thought of Ryan taking the piss out of her.

"Yes, that was me, I am very sorry," she said, her intolerance towards the imbecile before her mounting by the second.

The two boys lapsed into conversation and from eavesdropping Eimear was able to establish that Ryan was the ski host in Cartman's hotel. Not that she had any clue what a ski host did mind, but it sure as hell sounded better than an underwater bloody ceramic technician.

Oh God, she realised. I have a full-blown crush on this man.

Her mind wandered; she visualised them skiing together (for the sake of the dream, she skied with poise and style without falling over once); kissing beneath the clear, starry, French sky; laughing together in the bar with a group of friends as he gave her a small smile behind his pint, the sort of smile that those in love really share; some more kissing; a little bit of touching... (she spent quite a while imagining that scene, blushing slightly while she did); introducing him to her parents (who loved him instantly); meeting his parents (who loved her instantly); getting married; children; them as an elderly couple doing the crossword on a bench in the park whilst watching their grandchildren play....

"Yeah so, better go."

She was brought back to earth with a bang.

"Don't go," she yelped, a little bit too enthusiastically. Both guys stared at her.

"Um... look, I owe you for earlier. Would you like to join us for a drink? Will give us a chance to get to know each other and maybe we can sort out the details of the van?" And with that, she stood up, succeeded in knocking over yet another glass and as she tried to catch it, her hand brushed against his stomach.

Oh my God! It was like a wall, he owned a washboard torso. Her knees went weak on impact. Nice eyes and a nice stomach. God was testing her will-power.

"Accidental Eimear, I would love to stay for a drink," he said in his now calm Dublin tones with a grin which revealed the most beautiful set of teeth. She found herself mesmerised by them and could have sworn one of them even twinkled.

"I am afraid I can't, I have to get up early to ski with the guests in the morning so I better get back. Mike, see you back at the flat. Accidental Eimear, I'll text you with the details when I get the wing mirror sorted. À demain!"

"So what does he have to do exactly?" She asked, her eyes glued to his retreating backside.

"He has to ski with the guests and show them the resort," Cartman responded, apparently oblivious to her infatuation with his colleague. "God, it gets him in with the lady guests, let me tell you," he informed her with a cheesy and slightly sleazy wink.

Slags. Bitches. Eimear's dreams were suddenly shattered and images of watching grandchildren play in the park disappeared through the air like wispy smoke. The now grumpy Eimear drained the last few mouthfuls from her glass and got up to buy another one. "Want one?" she snapped, not even bothering to hide her hostility towards Cartman or, now she knew his real name, use it. His South Park name just seemed more fitting somehow.

She made her way to the bar, no longer caring that she had to be careful for her ski lesson the next day but an angry voice made her halt in her tracks.

"Eimear Barbara Moira O'Driscoll, you stop right there."

Party pooper Michelle had arrived.

"Mitch, you promised never to utter my confirmation name or my middle name for that matter in public! That isn't fair!"

"Neither is the fact that it is 11.30 at night and I have had to put my ski gear on over my pyjamas to make sure you are home in time for your ski lesson tomorrow. Now you are going to have to tear yourself away from your new love and come with me."

With that, Michelle turned to Cartman to apologise for dragging his date away, barely even cracking a smile at the sight of him. She picked up Eimear's ski jacket from her stool, grabbed her friend's hand and escorted her from the bar, out into the snowy night.

CHAPTER 10

Eimear hurt all over. Muscles she didn't even know existed ached. As she added the shallot onions to her beef casserole and stirred them into the already brimming pot, she winced as her arms ached with the effort. She would never be able to move with ease again.

Her first ski lesson had certainly been an interesting experience, from learning how to dress appropriately to the act of skiing itself. Dressing herself, this basic skill, even with all of her scattiness, was not normally an issue yet it proved to be far more complex than she had ever expected. When tackling ski boots, Eimear felt like a child who was learning to tie shoe laces correctly again. First was the convoluted task of getting her feet, which were enlarged dramatically by the thickness of her ski socks, into boots which looked like they had been built for Robocop himself. It was as though she was trying to wedge her feet into jam jars. No amount of stomping or hyperventilating led to the required result and eventually, she had to lie on the bottom bunk whilst Michelle aggressively manoeuvred them onto her feet. When they were finally on and each tightly secured buckle had imprisoned her foot into its plastic jail, she had attempted to walk in them. It was like wading through deep water with blocks of cement on her feet.

Next, she had learnt that the normal way of getting to the ski resort, which was a few thousand metres above the town, was to travel in what was quite appropriately called a 'ski bubble'. The journey alone had been enough to make her want to hang up her rented ski poles for life. As the bubble had ascended a cliff face, Eimear had chosen to stand right in the middle of the floor, a spot which was as far away from the windows as possible so that she could be in denial about how far above the ground she really was.

However, she could not prevent her eyes from drifting towards the skylight to the skinny wires above which were responsible for carting the bubble, also known as the telepherique, to the top of the mountain and ultimately, preventing her from hurtling to her death.

Then there was the lesson itself; the first move she learnt was the snow plough, a move where skis are positioned to form the top two sides of an equilateral triangle. This manoeuvre would apparently be her lifesaver as it gave skiers the ability to ski any gradient slowly whilst maintaining absolute control. After a few minutes of practising, Eimear was quickly identified as the runt of the litter by her ski instructor and consequently, received a lot of unwelcome attention for the remainder of the lesson.

Whilst Eimear found the snow plough to be a fantastic move in theory, its effectiveness depended on the skier's ability to actually execute the move and after failing to use it appropriately, she quickly discovered an even better method to slow down and stop. Find the softest looking patch of snow or snow drift and throw oneself onto it, a move which worked effectively every time. Although she had initially been scared of falling she had quickly overcome her fear when faced with the option of landing in soft snow or hurtling down the mountain Bridget Jones style. Landing on her backside looked like the more attractive option and the move quite quickly became her speciality.

There was just one problem. The manoeuvre was hindered somewhat by her instructor's determination to make her ski down a slope properly and every time she threw herself into her chosen mound of snow, a strong pair of arms would sift through it, find a part of her body to grab onto and remove her from it with extreme ease. She would then be plonked upright on her skis and quite against her will, dragged along the snow until she found herself, once again, on the precipice of the piste.

Skiing, she had decided, was her nemesis and finding love for it was definitely going to be a work in progress.

Unfortunately, the sport itself was not the only challenge she had had to contend with. There was also the problem of mounting a little delight known as chair lifts. These particular seats were, Eimear decided, the most bizarre-looking things she had ever set her eyes on. The metal chair lifts were scattered at various points throughout the ski resort and were used as a means to transport skiers from the bottom to the top of various ski runs. The legless, park-bench-shaped seats were suspended in mid-air from skinny wires which were strung from telegraph pole to telegraph pole, with nothing but a horizontal metal bar from one end of the seat to the other to keep their users 'strapped in'.

When François, her teacher, had decided that the majority of the class had mastered the snow plough, he had moved them on from the basic, wheelchair-shaped ramp they had been practising on to their first ski run.

"Don't worry Eimear," François had shouted over to her as she struggled to align her skis in the correct equilateral position. In her determination to not cross her skis over at the front, something which would result in her face-planting the snow, she neglected the back of her skis. They had slowly slipped further and further apart, causing her legs to splay like Bambi when he first took to ice. Her family's pet name for her had never been so apt. "I will assist you. Come, come."

The class had to plough towards the nearest ski lift, practising their new skill as they did. Eimear attempted to mimic her class mates whilst clutching onto François's arm for her dear life. Juggling skis, poles, ski passes, balance and dignity, each beginner cautiously swiped themselves through the turnstile. In groups of three, they made their way towards the benches, slowly mounted them when it was their turn and were whisked away into the ether.

With François's help, Eimear had managed to sit on the lift easily enough. Dismounting had not been as successful and she had made François work for his money as she'd put him in a headlock to save her from falling on her derrière.

After an hour of falling without style, ski lifts and holding onto poles which, quite frankly, she didn't see the point of, Eimear was knackered and, fed up of constantly being last in the class, had sworn she would never ski again. Unfortunately, Michelle and the rest of the team appeared to be in cahoots with François and had made a concerted effort since her first lesson to drag her out on the snowy ski runs whenever they could.

Her current aches and pains were attributable to her most

recent accident. She had ended up being tangled in a safety net which was positioned at the edge of a piste, designed to prevent wayward skiers from hurtling over the edge of a cliff into the deathly abyss below. Once she had been freed from her netted captor, she had made a hysterical phone call to her mother, begging her to take out life insurance in her name immediately as her death was sure to be imminent so her family might as well benefit from it. She had then clipped off her skis, flung them over her shoulder and stomped (as best as she could in ski boots) all the way down the piste to the large ski bubble and had descended to relative safety.

Thank God for the view, she thought, as she threw the last few ingredients into her simmering pot. It is the only thing worth travelling up that infernal bubble for.

The first time she had travelled up in the telepherique and had reached the centre of the resort, she had momentarily forgotten her nerves. The view was breath-taking. Mountain peaks lined the horizon, their mountain faces gleaming in the sun. Some surfaces had been carefully crafted into tidy ski runs whilst others had been left in their naturally rugged state. She had been almost blinded by the surrounding glistening snow as the sunlight bounced off of it, making the landscape appear as though it twinkled. Opposite the main ski station (or, as the locals called it, telepherique station) in the centre of the resort, she had spotted a number of bars, each one with an exotic-sounding French name. Different popular songs could be heard blasting out of their speakers for the customers or passing skiers to enjoy and, despite the cold, the decking outside each of the bars had been bustling with people lounging in deck chairs, enjoying the sunshine whilst sipping Vin Chaud, Genepi or other popular alpine drinks.

It was so beautiful, she had wanted to have a Julie Andrews moment from the Sound of Music, throw her arms out as wide as they would go and start spinning on the spot whilst singing at the top of her voice.

Her many layers had prevented her from doing so as they restricted her movement and she feared any movement, let alone sudden ones, would result in her falling over. Choosing caution over dramatics, she had decided to stay rooted on the spot until it was completely necessary to move.

Even when she had been swinging from her hated legless-park-bench ski lifts, angry at whichever of her team mates was making her face her newly developed skiing fear, her breath would be taken away by the view. She had never seen anything so stunning.

Michelle's voice brought her back to reality; "Are those canapés ready?"

Eimear scowled. Her best friend insisted on speaking to her in that damn Cartman accent ever since she had been reduced to tears on hearing about Eimear's not so successful date. Mitch thought she was hilarious; Eimear was not so sure.

"Yes," Eimear responded through gritted teeth, "the main is just about ready too. Have you sorted the starter and dessert?" she asked as the front door opened and the sound of their guests stomping excess snow off their boots and onto the front door mat rang through the air.

Each chalet host couple had to cook a four-course meal for their guests, including canapés, and serve as much house wine as their group desired. Much to the girls' delight, they were allowed to join the guests at the table to eat. Even more to their pleasure, when it wasn't their turn to drive the van back to the staff accommodation which was situated quite a bit away from the chalets, they were allowed to join in the drinking.

When Eimear and Michelle had seen their first group of visitors pull up in the minivan outside of their chalet, they had both been petrified. They had no idea whether they would be credible chalet hosts, if they would be able to look after the guests properly or even if the visitors would leave their chalet alive after they had sampled the girls' cooking. Even more terrifying, this particular group was going to be with them for longer than the normal one week visitation period as they had booked in to stay over Christmas and New Year. If they hated each other, they would be enduring it for a while. But Michelle and Eimear need not have worried. The Harpers were a lovely, fun family, who appreciated that it was their first time away from home so tried to distract them from any feeling of homesickness which they might have. Even though they had only been there for a few days, already both Eimear and Michelle were very fond of them and had arrived earlier than required a few times in order to play a few rounds of Boggle with them before they had to start preparing the evening meal.

"Starter is a last-minute frying job, I am going to do the scallops. I made the mascarpone and lime cheese cake this morning so just need to check it has set," Michelle said, as she opened the fridge door to check on her mixture.

"Oh bollocks." Michelle had, at last, dropped the Cartman voice.

Eimear joined her friend with her head inside the fridge door to witness the gloopy mess that was their dessert.

"What are we going to do?" Eimear saw the panic in her friend's eyes and felt that this was her moment to shine, to prove that she was not an absolute wimp. Yes, she may not be able to ski but goddammit, she would not let her friend look like a fool with slushy dessert!

"Ok, don't panic! I will run next door and see if Emma and Mark have any cheese left over from their cheese dessert night. If not, I will run to the shops before they close to get some local cheeses and we will do that dessert instead. If I am not back in time, you start serving the canapés and get frying the scallops for the starter."

She grabbed her coat, the van keys and shoved on her slightly masculine-looking snow boots, wincing slightly as she did at the strain on her various muscles.

"I won't be long, good luck!"

And with that, Eimear headed off into the darkening night to try and save the meal.

CHAPTER 11

The neighbouring chalet did not have anything the girls could use, so Eimear hopped into the van and drove into town. Terrible as it was, she felt secretly relieved that for once, she was not the one who had messed up, as was so usually the case. This finally gave her the chance to do something right for Michelle who was always bailing her out of burning-food disasters, extracting the van from various snow drifts Eimear had decided to plough into or untangling her from ski nets and ski boots. She flicked through the radio stations and found a song which was a particular favourite of hers as it brought back fond memories from home. She started swaying behind the steering wheel in time with the music and as she danced, she glanced at the clock on the dashboard and saw she only had twenty minutes to get to the shops and purchase the emergency cheese course ingredients before they closed.

She knew there was a short cut nearby which she could take to ensure she would get to the shops in time but it was one that was usually avoided by the team. When heavy snow had fallen, the single-tracked, steep road was particularly difficult to journey as the snow ploughs were not too vigilant at clearing it.

Even though they had had quite a heavy snow fall a few days before, Eimear felt that recently, her driving had really improved and her new-found confidence behind the wheel led her to believe she could handle the heavy van up the treacherous road. But her cockiness was unwarranted – a few accident free journeys did not a proficient van-driver make.

The bottom of the steep incline came into sight. Remembering all she had learnt from watching her colleagues drive over the last few weeks, she put the van into a lower gear and put her foot down on the accelerator to both create a bit of speed and help her maintain momentum as she climbed the treacherous road.

She only noticed how much the vegetation was straining under the weight of snow when she was already half way up the hill. She was also struggling to judge where the edge of the road ended and the ditch began, so deep was the snow on the road. Panic started fluttering through her chest; it was enough to make her concentration slip and she loosened her grip on both the wheel and the clutch.

It was the worst thing she could have done. With momentum lost, the van lost its grip on the snow and started to slide back down the hill.

"Arse!" she exclaimed to the empty van as she pulled on the handbrake, causing the van to skid slightly before grinding to a halt. But still she did not completely deteriorate into a gibbering mess; instead, she sifted through the various bits of information her colleagues had thrown at her when she had asked to be educated about driving in the snow after her last snow drift incident.

She decided it would be best to try and take the hill at a steady speed again. Taking a deep breath, she put the van into reverse, released the handbrake and started to reverse the van down the road, intending to reach the flat at the bottom of the hill where she would be able to gain the needed momentum.

Thanks to her inability to reverse in a straight line, she felt the van suddenly dip and checked her wing mirrors to see what was going on. She was no longer heading towards the bottom of the hill but now seemed to have a yew tree attached to her back doors.

"Merde!" she exclaimed to the empty van once again, her limited French now encompassing expletives. "Fucky fucky fuck fuck!"

Cursing to herself some more, she hopped out of the van and instantly sank in snow. She waded around the van to look at the back wheel and, on seeing the damage, slumped. She had driven slightly off the road and into the ditch, succeeding in completely submerging the rear, driver wheel and wedging the back of the van against the foliage. She would be there all bloody night.

Sighing to herself, she thought she should call Michelle before she started digging the van out to let her know she would have to start serving dinner without her and, as she would definitely miss the shops, go next door to the chalet and beg for something as simple as fruit and ice cream for dessert. But as she returned to the driver's seat and started looking for her phone, a horrible realisation dawned upon her. She had left the chalet in such haste, she hadn't grabbed her bag which contained her phone as well as her ski gloves. Not only was she now stranded on this desolate road in the darkening night all by herself with no one knowing where she was, she was going to have to dig the stupid van out with her bare hands. Pneumonia and frost bite were certainly going to be paying her a visit.

She started to feel overwhelmed by the situation. She reached underneath the driver's seat, pulled out the snow chains and snow shovel, then returned to the submerged wheel. As she worked, she swapped hands for shovel every five minutes or so to better get the wedged snow out from behind the wheel. While she worked, the potential severity of the situation dawned on her.

It all got a bit too much; as the tears started to fall, Eimear found herself looking up at the star-filled sky and cast a prayer into the ether.

"Please God, I know I thought I was coming here on a bit of a man fest so have undoubtedly pissed you off but I have really been good so far. If you could reward this good behaviour by somehow saving me, I will be really appreciative. If you don't want to help me out, please have a word with Granny. She sort of has to keep an eye on me, being family and all." And with that, she buried her head in her frozen hands.

After a few minutes of despairing, she wiped the tears off her cheeks, took a deep breath, grabbed the snow chains and tried wrapping them around the wheel. But still the snow was too deep and she was unable to attach them properly. Frustrated that she had subjected her fingers to the risk of amputation for nothing, Eimear decided to try rocking the van backwards and forwards, a method which had worked for Mark when he had imprisoned the van in a deep snow drift outside his chalet.

She hopped into the driver's seat, started the engine and cranked up the heating to try and restore feeling into her hands. When the numbness subsided and she was able to move her fingers again, she put the gear stick into first and started pressing and releasing the clutch as she had seen her friends do. But she pressed the clutch too hard, causing the wheels to spin, trapping the van even further in the snow.

Eimear dropped her head onto the steering wheel and started to sob. Her predicament was hopeless; she was going to be stuck here all night. She was up a stupid back road in the middle of nowhere, with no hope of being found because anyone with even the smallest bit of sense would not drive along it in these conditions. She realised she had two choices; either abandon the van to try and find help or stick with it and hope that Michelle knew her well enough to realise the stupid mistake she had made and send help. She remembered an evening she had spent watching a documentary with her dad about ways of surviving when stuck in the wilderness. The first thing the presenter had said as he gazed down the camera lens, not a flicker of a smile or personality, was, "The worst thing you could do is leave your car. Always stay with the vehicle; it provides you with shelter and is an obvious landmark for the rescue party to look for. NEVER LEAVE THE VEHICLE."

Eimear felt slightly better after remembering that authoritative voice, but her relief was short lived somewhat when she remembered that the conditions the explorers were lost in were usually warm, balmy deserts. Not sub-zero conditions which, if exposed to for long enough, would cause imminent death.

Oh Jesus, Eimear thought, sobbing harder now. I am going to die tonight! Tomorrow morning or maybe even months from now if the road is too bad to travel down, they will find my body perfectly preserved in the snow. My mother is going to be devastated. I wonder who will come to my funeral?

Eimear found herself oddly captivated by her final thought and, sobbing subsided, found herself slightly distracted as she tried to work out who would attend her burial.

A knock at the window gave her the fright of her life and brought her crashing out of her trance. Through the closed window, she heard the words,

"Oh Jesus, I should have guessed it would be you holding up the whole bloody road."

Eimear froze.

Please God, please don't be so cruel as to let it be him. Come on now, I know I wanted help but this is just mean, she thought to herself, eyes scrunched so tight they hurt, so desperate was she to have her stern words with God be well and truly received.

Aware that her nose was dribbling and that she looked an awful mess after all of the sobbing, Eimear tried to surreptitiously wipe her face against her sleeve to remove any of the gloop that may be there, then slowly raised her face.

God? You are a right ol' dick sometimes, do you know that? Out of all of the people you could have sent me in L'Homme, you chose to send him. You are supposed to be nice to me, being one of your chosen people, being Irish and all, she thought to herself as she looked into the beautiful blue eyes of the man before her.

"Howya?" she said as she lowered her window and gave Ryan a watery, toothy grin.

"Having a bit of trouble are we?" Ryan asked, his mesmeric eyes sparkling with the hilarity of finding a dejected, slumped Eimear stuck in a ditch.

Eyes filling once again, Eimear merely nodded, her bottom lip quivering with the effort of holding back the sobs.

"Out you get," he ordered, opening the door and holding out his hand to help her jump down from her seat.

Without a word of explanation, Ryan climbed into the driver's seat, turned the engine back on and started rocking the van backwards and forwards.

Within seconds, he had removed the van from its snowy vortex, had realigned the van so it pointed in the correct direction and was backing it to the bottom of the road.

Gobsmacked, it took Eimear a few seconds to register what was happening, so smooth had the rescue mission been. When she realised she was no longer stranded, she picked up the snow chain and shovel and ran down the hill after her retreating van.

"So what stunt were you trying to pull?" Ryan asked as the breathless Eimear eventually materialised at the passenger window.

"I needed cheese!" Was all she could manage before she doubled over, clutching the piercing cramp in her side.

"And you were hoping to find it in the ditch?"

She shook her head, held up her finger to request a moment and, when she had gathered her wits, straightened up to explain all about Michelle's dessert disaster and how her cunning plan to save time had not been so cunning after all.

"But now I am late, Michelle won't know what has happened to me and I am going to return to the chalet with nothing." The panic was evident in Eimear's voice as she finished her story.

"Well Accidental Eimear, it looks as though I am your knight in shining armour. My hotel is not too far from the top of the hill you so epically failed to climb. I was on my way out to pick up some guests who are late to dinner as they have lost all sense of time thanks to the liquid lunch they have been consuming for the last eight hours. I could see someone was stuck further down this lane which, by the way, no one in their right mind would travel in these conditions. You know the main road is just there don't you? Anyway, I decided to walk along to see if I could help. How about I walk back up, ask the chef if you could steal some of the cheese from the kitchen for tonight and while I am gone, you call your phone from mine and hope that Michelle hears it so you can explain what has happened?"

Eimear watched his retreating back as she waited for Michelle to pick up her phone. While she listened to the dial tone, a new romantic scenario materialised in her mind. In it, she and her skis were no longer being excavated from deep snow drifts by a handsome, French, ski-instructing knight. Now, she and her van were being exhumed out of snow drifts by a cheese-bearing, Irish, ski host with piercing blue eyes. As the day dream progressed, she was no longer being whisked away and romanced by a man that did not sound too dissimilar from Lumière from Beauty and the Beast. Now, she was being romanced in the arms of a particular Irish man, one with weak-knee-inducing blue eyes and the ability to turn up when Eimear was causing destruction.

This was one dream that had the potential to come true.

CHAPTER 12

Eimear applied the last of her mascara, took a sip of her wine which she had courtesy of the chalet's wine stock and had a look at her reflection in the tiny mirror that hung on the back of the door. Satisfied with what she saw, she grabbed her brimming wine glass and the bottle of wine and joined the rest of her team in the staff living room.

The girls realised that they had been well and truly spoilt with the Harpers. They had been fun, polite, friendly and had made being away from home on Christmas day bearable for the girls. They had even celebrated the first time Eimear managed to get down a blue run without falling over.

Long gone were the days when Eimear would ski across the piste and purposefully aim for a fluffy-looking snow drift to crash into. No longer would she, once she had collided with her chosen buffer, lie in a compromising position on the snow whilst manoeuvring her skis to point to the opposite side of the ski run. No longer did she need to struggle into the standing position once her skis were pointing the right way, ski across to the other side of the piste and crash into her next chosen snow drift.

Now, she could successfully snow plough, albeit slowly, all the way to the bottom of the piste without throwing herself to the ground the moment she got scared.

Empathising with her sense of achievement, the guests celebrated her delight by getting the two girls very intoxicated during dinner. A lot of courses were burnt that evening.

Oh how both Eimear and Michelle missed them, even though two weeks had passed after their sorrowful departure. This sense of loss had only been heightened as both they and the remainder of the team had experienced a number of particularly difficult guests since Christmas.

Eimear was starting to realise that her role as chalet host was much more than just cooking and cleaning for guests; apparently she was also expected to pander to her guests' every whim no matter how ridiculous. Two of her current guests appeared to be particularly fond of the abnormal and did not think any task too strange for the girls. Until their arrival, Eimear had always thought that a spoon was just a spoon. She knew they came in different shapes and sizes but even so, she did not think their physical appearance ever detracted from their function as a working spoon. Not once did she ever imagine that the bendiness of a spoon's handle could affect the way one ate their leek and potato soup. Or at least that was until Mrs Charlotte Bates, the current bane of the girls' lives, arrived. Whilst eating the first starter of her week-long stay, she complained that the handle of her soup spoon was too bendy, that she could not possibly be expected to eat soup with it and demanded that it be replaced immediately.

Unfortunately, this was not the only quirky personality flaw the dreaded Mrs Charlotte Bates had displayed in the first few days since she had arrived. At dinner the following night, she had dropped her knife on the dining room floor. As the sound of the metal hitting the tiles rang out through the dining room, she had screamed in pure terror. Staring at the dropped knife, she frantically summoned Michelle over and requested that the chalet host picked up the knife for her. Michelle met the request with a slightly hostile look, causing the terrified guest to explain that she could not pick it up herself as to do so would inflict many years of bad luck upon her. Michelle, her face now looking dubious, had passed the irascible guest the fallen knife and reassured her that it was quite possible to replace it with a new one, an offer which was met with disdain. Charlotte insisted that the only way to ensure the bad luck was destroyed was to continue using the salvaged dirty implement, now reunited with her hand.

Eimear too suffered at the hand of her superstitious guest's idiosyncrasies when asked to pass the salt. As she had attempted to put the salt cellar into Mrs Bates' hand, her nervous guest had let out an anxious squeal and had demanded that Eimear put the salt on the table in front of her instead of into her hand. Apparently, to accept it directly from another human hand would, once again, inflict years of bad luck on her.

Who needs Catholicism to rebel against when you have superstitions like this? Eimear had wondered as she placed the salt on the table and watched Charlotte's quivering hand pick it up, causing the salt to fall in uneven clumps all over the guest's plate, ruining the meal the girls had worked so hard to prepare.

But it was Charlotte's rant at dinner that evening that had finally pushed the girls over the edge, causing them to bully the rest of the team into having a much needed good night out to help them forget the lunacy of their guests.

In the middle of every week, Lucy had a meeting with each chalet to inform the hosts of any dietary requirements their next set of guests had. On learning that a Mrs Charlotte Bates did not like pork, the girls changed their food plan so it accommodated their guest's requests; but the girls had not anticipated that this woman's dietary requirements were far more problematic than a mere dislike of pork. This woman was all kinds of crazy.

When bacon was on the menu for breakfast for all of the other guests, Mr Bates had asked for porridge to be taken up to his wife in the bedroom and that all doors and windows to the downstairs area were kept closed so that the smell of the meat sizzling in the frying pan did not seep throughout the chalet.

"She has a very delicate stomach," he commented, as he backed out of the kitchen, one hand clutching the porridge while closing the door with the other.

Having learnt to 'love thy neighbour' at school, the girls merely did nothing more than roll their eyes. They knew they should try to be tolerant and celebrate their differences. However, there was nothing in the Bible telling them they could not find their present guest to be an irritating fool whom they both secretly wished would fall off a cliff and so continued cooking bacon for the remainder of their guests in slightly hostile silence.

But the same thing happened again at dinner and once again, while the rest of the guests ate their pork chops with apple and thyme sauce at the dinner table, Mrs Bates' plain chicken was served in her room. Unlike at breakfast, Mr Bates had decided to sit with the guests at dinner instead of eating with his wife in their room. When the main course was served, the oppressed husband pushed his pork chop around his plate nervously, then whispered guiltily,

"She will kill me if I eat this..."

After a few more minutes of pushing the morsel around his plate, he shrugged before consuming the pork chop with ravenous desire and lust in his eyes.

Poor deprived, burdened sod, Eimear had thought sympathetically as she watched him salivate over the rapidly diminishing carcass, her tolerance of Mrs Bates' behaviour declining even further.

But after dinner, both Eimear's and Michelle's patience levels plummeted. Having decided that the smell of pork had finally left the kitchen, the wayward crazy guest left the safe confines of her room and joined the remainder of the chalet's occupants for after-dinner games. The suggestions of Scrabble, snakes and ladders and gin rummy had been met with half-hearted enthusiasm so the girls had rooted around in the games cupboard before finding 'Pass the Pigs', a game which was met with far more gusto.

Eimear explained the rules of the game, "... So points are rewarded to the thrower depending on the final resting position of the two small rubber pigs..."

A small cough interrupted her.

"I can't play that," Charlotte had interjected as she stared at the offending miniature pig-shaped dice resting on the table beside the score board. This unwelcome outburst was delivered with a deathly stare at Eimear who had purposely refused to acknowledge her cough.

"Why not?" Michelle challenged, somewhat politely although a note of exasperation could be heard by all.

"Because they are pigs," the grumbler responded with a sarcastic tone, as though Michelle's question was completely moronic.

"Ok.... But I still don't see the problem," Eimear joined in.

"Pork comes from pigs... I do not like pigs."

Silence descended on the room. The other guests avoided eye contact with one another, knowing that hysterical laughter would erupt should their eyes meet.

"But they aren't real pigs," responded Eimear after what felt like a lifetime. Her voice was no longer polite but was laced with irritation. "They are just little bits of rubber in the shape of pigs."

"Nevertheless," Mrs Bates said haughtily, "I shall not be participating in this game. Come Roger, you will not be touching them either."

And with that, Mrs Charlotte Bates swept out of the dining room dragging her poor, spineless husband behind her.

As the door was slammed shut on their retreating backs and the remainder of the guests erupted into frenzied laughter, Eimear's and Michelle's eyes had met across the dinner table with a silent agreement.

Tonight, they were hitting the town. Hard.

It had not taken much to persuade the rest of the team and when Eimear walked into the dining room with her wine in tow, the party was already in full swing. She didn't know what it was about doing a ski season but she had noticed a definite regression in the mental ages of her male colleagues since the start of their time in France.

Rory and Andrew were jumping from armchair to armchair while rocking out with their air guitars to Guns n' Roses' 'Sweet Child of Mine'. Mark, meanwhile, was flicking the light switch on and off to try and create a disco feel to the room. The girls sat, somewhat sedately in comparison, around the room, swigging out of their stolen wine bottles and casually but quickly moving their legs whenever it looked like they were going to be crushed by one of the flying bodies.

Eimear sat in between Leanne and Emma and listened to them complain about the guests currently in their chalets while watching the boys who were now dry-humping one another in an obscurely-shaped three way.

Something about the playful and childlike behaviour emanating from the grown men before her made Eimear think of Peter Pan's Neverland and his Lost Boys. As a child, Eimear had loved watching the Disney adaptation of this film and, whenever she and her brothers had re-enacted it, she always dressed up as Wendy. While her brothers always swore they too would be like the Lost Boys and would never grow up, utterly convinced that they would maintain their childhood innocence and frivolity forever, Eimear had sworn that she would one day grow up and have her own family to look after, just like Wendy Darling.

As she watched the three guys before her now give one another wedges, she decided they, and even the men she met in the resort every day, were no different from the Lost Boys. L'Homme was the real life Neverland for every man; it was the tangible equivalent of the land of eternal youth and in it every man was encouraged to re-discover their inner child. Women, on the other hand, behaved very much like Wendy Darling; although they had fun for the period they were in L'Homme, the vast majority of them looked forward to leaving its timeless bubble and returning to normality. Eimear did not know why it did not affect women in the same way but as she watched her female colleagues observe their boyfriends' behaviours with complete indifference, she resigned herself to the common belief that men and women were, and always would be, from completely different planets.

Her phone beeped, bringing her out of her reflective bubble. Reading the message she rolled her eyes and passed her phone to the other girls, encouraging them to read it so she could share her frustration with them.

"We are never off duty!" she exclaimed as Michelle took the phone off Ruth so she could read it too. Michelle and Eimear had warned Lucy that putting two separate holiday groups under one roof would cause problems, especially if they did not get on. The text message she had received was from the fun group of guests who were now complaining that the 'pork haters' were 'doing their head in' and could the two girls please find them all rooms in another of the company's chalets?

"Your day off started the moment you guys left the chalet for the night," Emma said as Eimear started drafting a response. "It isn't your problem until you go back in on Thursday morning."

"I know, but these guys are not too bad and honestly, I feel their pain. I could not spend any more time in the chalet than necessary because the Bates couple really are crazy. I will let them know that I will contact Lucy and Ian in the morning and see what we can do."

Eimear's phone beeped almost instantaneously after she clicked 'Send'. Surprised to get a response from the guests so quickly, she clicked 'Read' without acknowledging who the sender was.

But it wasn't from her guests.

'Thanks for sorting the wing mirror, checked my bank account online today and saw you had transferred the money.

Maybe see you out tonight for a few to celebrate the newest part of my van? R xx'

Eimear froze in her seat; he was going to be out tonight. She downed the last of the wine in her bottle and bellowed,

"Everybody OUT NOW. It is time to GO!"

Excitement coursed through her body as she started hustling all of her friends out of their seats and extracted the boys from their various tantric positions. It was not that she wanted anything to happen with Ryan, she tried to convince herself, he was just a friend. But, you know, it would be rude to keep her knight waiting. With a new-found enthusiasm for the night, Eimear skipped to her room to grab her ski jacket. Who knew where the night could take her?

CHAPTER 13

Once an impatient Eimear had managed to prise Mark away from his light-flicking home disco, a position he had quickly resumed once prevented from sexually abusing his male colleagues, and the remainder of the team had drunk all of their looted wine, she ran around all of their rooms grabbing their thick coats. When they were all appropriately dressed and boozed up, they headed into town.

The norm had become that they all drank chalet wine in The Palace to save money. Unfortunately, this resulted in them becoing so drunk in their staff accommodation, they no longer thought that saving money was an issue and would withdraw a 'reasonable' amount from their bank accounts. This 'reasonable' amount, it would transpire the next morning, would be their entire (pitiful) weekly wages, an action which was always met with a lot of regret. But none of this would matter as they staggered towards the local seasonaire bar, Binky's. As most seasonal workers had Wednesday off, the most popular night out was Tuesday and true to the norm, the bar and dance floor were packed to the brim.

As the team entered, they nodded to the bouncer and made their way to the bar whilst Eimear quickly scanned the crowd for any sign of Ryan. She and Michelle had made friends with Henry, one of the French bar men, a few weeks before and had found him to be a particularly helpful alibi. It also helped that he fancied the pants off Michelle and so enjoyed plying the two girls with free drinks in the hope that Michelle would give him more attention. True to form, the moment he caught sight of the two girls hanging over the bar, he immediately made his way over to them and served the whole team, ignoring the complaints of those who had been waiting a while. Drinks bought and a complimentary round of shots from Henry downed, the team scattered, the guys continuing to prop up the bar whilst the women headed to the dance floor.

Within minutes, the girls had been attacked by a swarm of

Bobs. A Bob, whose over-the-top baggy fashion sense led him to be categorised as a 'Yo' within the resort, targeted Eimear and made his way through the crowd towards her, his face straining with the concentration of reaching his prey.

Not long after moving to L'Homme, Eimear had noticed a 'fashion' that appeared to have infested the resort, a fashion which was so baggy it made a morbidly obese individual look anorexic. It was a fashion which knew no bounds and gave one status in any ski resort. This fashion, she learnt, was known as 'The Rise of the Yos'.

It quickly became apparent that, in normal society, Yos would be considered the outcasts. Against all odds, when submerged in the bubble that is skiing Neverland, these overdressed buffoons were 'cool'. Yos were the kids who used to sit at the back of the classroom with fringes down to their noses and spots for friends. These were the kids who, in their teenage years, rebelled against their parents and society by haunting library steps with their skateboards and their BMX bikes. Playing around in public places meant they could not be controlled; they were free spirits and would flip their boards night and day to show they were 'sticking it to The Man'. As old grannies left the library with their new books piled under one arm, these revolutionaries would scoot off in front of the poor unsuspecting pensioners on their wheeled toy of choice and leap off the top step whilst performing a 'varial kick flip'. On landing, they would look over their shoulder to see the look of astonishment on the innocent bystander's face while chuckling to themselves that doing those jumps in front of elderly people made them so 'rad'. Who knew that these were the very same people who would be setting trends and developing groupies in L'Homme?

Yos took the bagginess of a normal Bob to a whole new and more extreme level; a Yo's hat would be branded with some 'name drop' label that was likely to go in and out of fashion as quickly as it took a Bob to spot a new victim. Their hair resembled that of Prince Charming's from Shrek; long, wavy and carefully crafted to get that 'cool but ruffled' look. Their faces were partially covered with bum fluff which had been vigilantly sculptured into a beard of some description; the better the facial carving the further they were into their post-adolescence phase. When they didn't have a ski jacket that dropped below their knees, they were likely to don a hoodie which looked more like a dress than a jumper. As if that wasn't enough, this would all be covered with a basketball vest which swept the ground. Their ski trousers (salopettes) would be better fitted to the saggy baggy elephant than a human and could normally be located just south of their butt cheeks whilst being 'kept up' with a huge belt.

The Yo-Bob started his seduction dance, circulating Eimear with a little bit of muscle flexing here, a slight clench of the butt cheek there, a cheeky smile thrown in for good measure. Whilst she tried to ignore his moves, she found her eyes being strangely captivated by this particular Yo-Bob's belt.

It was ginormous, as though the very size of it was supposed to aid the Yo-Bob in mesmerising his victims, thereby rendering them incapacitated and perfect for the Yo-Bob to strike.

As this baggy Yo-Bob continued marking his territory, she found herself speculating whether the size of the belt was an indication of what really lay beneath, or whether it was in fact compensating for something. Perhaps this Yo-Bob felt a gargantuan beacon on his groin was necessary to attract the attention of the opposite sex as his actual body would not. Mid-thought, Eimear saw him pull up his trousers which had started to slide further down his legs in the middle of his routine, distracting her attention from his groin to his now exposed bottom. As she studied his derrière, she came to the conclusion that the 'Yo' look did not look cool, comfortable, dignified or, most importantly, sexy. Quite the contrary in fact; it just made the wearer look as though they had a pole stuck up their backside as, to ensure he did not lose his trousers completely to gravity, the Yo-Bob before her had to circle her with a waddle. Although she knew the baggier the clothes, the 'cooler' and 'better' a skier or snowboarder someone was, Eimear thought the look screamed 'I have to wear my obese cousin's hand-me-down ski clothes as I am too poor to buy my own.'

As the waddling dance continued, Eimear was reminded of an

article she once discovered in The Times. The interviewer, who had been speaking to those who had been through the jail system, suggested that, historically, homosexual inmates in the prison system wore their trousers around the base of their butt as it flaunted or implied willingness to partake in that kind of activity. She sniggered to herself as she was reminded of this as she watched Yo-Bob and wondered if he knew he was actually sending out a very different message from, 'I am submerged in bagginess so you know what a cool, amazing individual I am.'

As the attempt to woo her through his moves reached a frenzied climax, he leant in to deliver the expected fateful line,

"I am just like the Titanic, I always go down on the first date. So…" he winked, "how would you like me to make your breakfast for you in the morning?"

A double whammy. Eimear swallowed the little amount of vomit that had risen in the back of her throat but decided to overlook the appalling line. Underneath all of that bagginess and bum fluff she thought he was probably quite a nice person. Her ridiculous naivety was most likely attributable to her alcohol-induced haze and because she was annoyed at herself for being so bothered that she still could not see Ryan in the crowd. Gazing upon the Yo-Bob for a while she decided he was not a complete munter and felt as though she should chat to him for a while as a reward for his hunting stamina. But after ten minutes of strained conversation by which time her tolerance had reached its peak, a ten minutes she realised she would never get back, she made her excuses and joined the rest of her friends on the dance floor's stage. But Yo-Bob was not so easy to deter and followed her whilst thrusting his hips in time to the music in the hope that breaking out some more of his serious moves would definitely score him a mate for the night.

Unbeknown to Eimear, she had attracted a particularly loony Yo-Bob.

As the thrusting and boogying continued, a holiday-maker, easily spotted by the matching t-shirt he and his friends were wearing with their nicknames and the slogan "Lads on Tour" emblazoned on the back, caught sight of Yo-Bob's overly large, labelled hat. Like a child who yearns for a forbidden lollipop, he reached out and in one swift motion, removed it from Yo-Bob's head. His goofy, smug grin spread across his drunken face as he held his stolen prize up for all of his friends to see, his pride apparent. "Look what I have coveted," it screamed, "I have a stupid baggy hat all of my own!"

As the hat was dangled before Yo-Bob's face by the chuckling punter in what was a particularly antagonistic move, Yo-Bob grabbed the unsuspecting man's shirt, pulled his face towards him and appeared to whisper something into his ear.

But as the punter pulled away, Eimear covered her mouth in shock.

His ear was covered in blood.

Yo-Bob had bitten his ear.

She wasn't sure if imitating Mike Tyson and resorting to cannibalism was a stunt Yo-Bob had pulled to try to show off his masculinity in a final attempt to impress her. Maybe he was just mad. Whatever his excuse, she sure as hell knew she did not want to stick around and find out.

She ran off the dance floor, leaving her friends to deal with the whimpering punter and submerged herself in a crowd next to the bar in the hope that Yo-Bob would not be able to find her. As she did so, she bumped into someone's drink, spilling the contents of it all over her.

"Jesus Christ, when disaster is happening in this town I can now just about guarantee you are behind it. First my wing mirror, then you clog up my road and now you destroy my drink. Are you accident prone or what?"

That voice. Eimear's knees weakened at hearing the gentle dulcet tones of the man she had a habit of, sometimes literally, bumping into when she was doing something stupid. God she felt pathetic, letting a man affect her this way. But those eyes, those stunningly beautiful, drowning blue eyes. The already weakened knees buckled ever so slightly.

"Sup?" She said with a slight flick of her head, a move she thought made her look cool and indifferent in spite of the mayhem she had just caused to the front of his shirt.

"What's the rush?" he asked, now peeling his soaked shirt from his extremely well-chiselled torso. Eimear tried to avert her eyes but failed miserably.

"Well... um... Mike Tyson is here," and at that, Eimear suddenly found herself crippled by laughter as the ridiculousness of what just happened dawned upon her. As laughter progressed to shoulder-shaking snorts, she thought she did not want this beautiful man to think she sounded like a pig so attempted to stifle her laughter. But the thought of pigs reminded her of those bloody guests of hers and she was off again, tears of laughter now joining her piggy look.

Not for the first time in Eimear's presence, Ryan looked perplexed.

When the laughter and honks from her nose eventually subsided, Ryan watching her all the while looking very bemused, she was able to explain about her guests and her most recent escapade with a Yo-Bob, gesturing behind her as she did.

"Well, there is a guy making a beeline for you, is that him?"

Eimear jumped, looked over her shoulder and groaned at the sight of Yo-Bob who was, indeed, ploughing through the crowd straight towards her.

"What's cookin' good lookin'?" Yo Bob had arrived. "Where did you go?"

Before Eimear had the chance to even open her mouth with a response, she felt a firm arm around her shoulders and she was whisked out of Yo-Bob's sight behind Ryan's broad shoulders. Although outraged that she had been deprived of the opportunity to tell Yo-Bob to do one herself, she felt secretly excited by Ryan's muscular arm around her shoulder.

"She's with me actually, that's what is 'cookin'. So if you don't mind, we will be on our way and you can get lost."

And with that, Ryan turned his back on the now speechless Yo-Bob who didn't look too dissimilar to a rabbit who had been caught in headlights, and gently hustled Eimear closer to the bar.

"I could have handled that myself you know," Eimear muttered grumpily, not wanting Ryan to think she was completely incapable. "I don't need a man to jump in and save me all the time."

"Eimear, it has nothing to do with being a man. I just know that guy's reputation and he is a particular level of low-life scum. I especially didn't want him speaking to you of all people like that. Anyway, I am starting to realise you often need a second pair of hands to help you out of these scrapes you manage to get yourself in to. Anyone with a bit of common sense would do, male or female. Now stop shooting me those evil looks and let's get a few drinks to celebrate my van's recovery and your close shave with Mike Tyson over there."

Eimear threw one final hostile look in his direction and leant along the bar in an attempt to look sultry and sexy. She was annoyed that he had intervened as she had always prided herself on being independent and not needing anyone, particularly a guy, to sort things out for her. Her stubborn side wanted to show him she was a good-looking, sophisticated woman, not a train wreck in need of charity. As she perfected her 'sensual look', she realised her arm was stuck to the bar thanks to the sticky Sambuca shot someone had knocked over. She peeled her skin off the wooden bar and tried to surreptitiously wipe the mess off her arm and onto her tights but heard Ryan try to stifle his sniggers behind her. Highly embarrassed, she caught Henry's eye and bought Ryan a number of drinks at once, partially as an apology for ruining yet another of his possessions but also to try and show him that, although she was a clumsy fool, she was a generous one who was skilled at acquiring alcoholic beverages quickly.

Drinks in their hands, they wandered through the bar and found an empty booth. While they drank, Eimear started to learn a little bit more about her knight; Ryan was twenty-three years old, was on his fifth ski season and like most Irish Catholics, he came from a very large family. They chatted about their skiing abilities, both Eimear's lack of and Ryan's love for the sport. As they talked about skiing, she could see the passion in his face and before long, realised that he was addicted to seasons. He launched into a monologue about the freedom he felt on the mountains, a freedom he had never felt at home being one of many siblings in a small house and that living in the happy bubble of a ski resort allowed him to forget about the world outside of the one he had created for himself. As his eyes lit up with excitement, Eimear's heart sank as she realised her knight was yet another Lost Boy.

"But I think this may be my last season though," he said, sadness filling his face. "My parents want me to go back to Dublin and get, as they call it, 'a proper job.'" He picked up his pint glass and drained the last of his drink. "Never mind, I will worry about that at the end of the season. Thanks for the drinks, if you want me to give you some skiing tips next time you are up the mountain like we discussed, send me a text. Have a good night."

As Eimear watched her lost knight walk away from her, a horrible realisation dawned upon her. She really liked this guy and that was the last thing she wanted. She had come on this season in the hope of finding some fun, but fun that had a definite end date and would not cause her to lose her head, something which she felt would be a certain if she chased Ryan. It was all just a bit too intimidating. She too downed the rest of her drink and went in search of her friends. It was time to go home.

CHAPTER 14

"Why won't you admit you like him?" Michelle asked, as she drained the boiled carrots in the colander and threw them into the pot in preparation for the carrot and coriander soup she was making. "Don't know why you feel the need to hide it from me, it is so bloody obvious. Every time he texts you to arrange a ski lesson your face immediately resembles a tomato."

Another cold week of January had passed since the crazy-haters-of-pork-for-no-apparent-reason had left and Eimear, so freaked out by the unexpected intensity of her feelings for Ryan, had decided that she would enter the wonderful world of denial. If she denied her emotions to everyone for long enough, it might just come true.

Unfortunately, this was becoming increasingly harder to do the more time she and Ryan spent together. She had taken him up on his offer of ski lessons the day after Binky's and they had met every day since for a couple of hours up the mountain. He tended to ski with his guests for a few hours, then ski with Eimear before returning to his guests for the rest of the afternoon. She had already noticed a significant progress in her skiing; she had been so determined to not show herself up that she had not only listened intently to Ryan's tips but had made a conscious effort to overcome her fear and put his ideas into practice.

In the space of a week, she had learnt to parallel ski, a move where the skis are placed side by side as opposed to snow plough where the skis meet at the top. She had even started to feel confident enough to point her skis straight down the mountain instead of working her way down the piste by skiing across it, side to side. Even though she was still quite clumsy with the moves and got scared when she picked up speed so would revert to skiing across the piste, she was really proud of the progress she was making, especially since January was not yet over and she thought it would take her months to get that far.

Ryan was kind in his praise and only that day had told her he was really pleased with her. She had tried to tell herself that the fluttering in her chest was the response to his praise and not because his fringe had flopped across his forehead at the time and she had wanted to stroke it to the side of his face.

Michelle too had noticed a change in Eimear's reaction to Ryan's name. With every lesson that passed, Eimear tended to flush more deeply anytime someone said something about him. Eimear poo-pooed her claim and would quickly change the conversation.

With the annoying guests gone, Eimear and Michelle had hoped for a better week but Lucy and Ian had placed three couples who did not know each other in their chalet and there was a social problem. The girls had to listen to a range of pointed comments from two nice, fun couples about the third couple who quickly became known to the girls as 'The Sex Pests'.

They had seemed rather unusual even when they first arrived at the chalet. Both of them were an odd shade of orange with teeth that had an unnatural whiteness. Mrs Sex Pest had an interesting ring around her jaw line suggesting that her tangoed skin was not quite dark enough for her face so it required ten or 20 extra layers of make-up to compensate. Her peroxide blonde hair had been backcombed within an inch of its life and made into a quiff. Her once pert, now somewhat sagging, wrinkled breasts were on display for all to see in a low-cut leopard print top. Unfortunately, her groin was also on show as she donned overly tight leggings on her bottom half, leaving little to the imagination. All of this was topped off with a pair of heels, completely inappropriate given their snow holiday, and a fur coat. Mark was certainly not impressed when he had to carry her from the minivan into the chalet on arrival as she had not wanted to ruin her shoes in the snow.

Mr Sex Pest arrived in a shiny velour tracksuit which was unzipped halfway down to reveal a hairy chest, decorated with a gold medallion. His forest-covered pecs made up for the lack of hair on his head which he had attempted to disguise with a carefully crafted combover.

The girls had liked them at first; they both seemed quite refreshingly down to earth. However, Eimear and Michelle quickly realised The Sex Pests were not their kind of people when they started harping on about how immigrants were the reason the economy was on the blink and that they should be made to pay for taking all of the good jobs. And this was all before the sex toys were discovered.

Where school had lacked in educating their girls about sex, their job as chalet hosts certainly made up for it. Michelle was not as uninformed as Eimear, having had a bit of a reputation at school, one which she took great pride in working on in the ski resort. In fact, there had been many a night after hitting the local club that Eimear had walked home without her roommate as Michelle went back to a Bob's house.

As for Eimear, other than 'the only contraception is to say No', a particular favourite of their R.E. teachers, the principal piece of advice she had received from school was to put a phone book on the lap of any man they intended to sit on to ensure appropriate distance was maintained between the opposite sexes' genitalia. She had been given some guidance at home; her mother had awkwardly taken her through the motions of what various contraceptive bits and bobs were but it had been such a traumatic conversation for them both, they had rushed through it and had never discussed it ever again.

Her brothers' sex talk had been left in the not-so-capable hands of their father, who had apparently done an even worse job of informing his boys of what one should and should not do when it came to sex. When her older brothers had learnt that Eimear had been given 'the talk', they had all hidden in the garden shed and compared notes; not on what they should do, just on how embarrassed their parents had been when talking to them. Like her, the boys had never discussed their sex education lesson with either of their parents again. However Eimear remembered the first time her oldest brother stayed out all night, much to her mother's disgust, an incident which had nearly led to her mother broaching the sex lesson again. When Donnacha sauntered back in at eleven o'clock the following morning, a girl's lipstick evident across his cheeks and on parts of his clothing, t-shirt askew and with the biggest grin on his face, her mother had lost the plot altogether and had lectured him on the dangers of casual sex despite his assertions that he really had just stayed over at his best friend's house. Much to the delight of the other siblings, mid-rant they overheard the line, one which had become a favourite of theirs and was still quoted to one another to this day – "An erect penis has no conscience!"

Oh how she and her other two brothers had howled as they sat on the landing listening to Donnacha stuttering helplessly as he received the most mortifying telling-off of his life time.

In spite of Eimear's sheltered sex life and Michelle's experienced one, both of them were quite astounded at the various instruments and level of, or in this case, lack of cleanliness of The Sex Pests' bedroom. The two girls had realised quite quickly that they could learn a lot about their guests from the way they left their rooms every morning when they went out to the slopes. Eimear and Michelle normally alternated who would clean the rooms every day while the other would bake the afternoon tea cake. However, the two girls decided they would tackle The Sex Pests' bedroom together after Eimear had nearly suffered a cardiac arrest when she went into their room on the first morning of their stay and found evidence of their active sex life everywhere. The memory of it still caused severe nausea.

As she tried to avoid the various items of clothing scattered across the floor, a dirty thong here, a skid-marked boxer there, she wish there had been a guide book to being a chalet host and the surprises one may find in the bedrooms of guests. She wished she had gone to a normal school and had been taught to put a condom on a banana or cucumber like everyone else so that what she saw in the bedroom would not have shocked her so much.

She wished her Catholic education had not left her so naive and innocent. But above all, she wished she had been warned about the type of guests who kept the other guests awake throughout the night with the sound of slapping skin and yelps as one or, sometimes (although according to the other guests, it happened rarely) even both, climaxed, a sound one of the other guests compared to howling wolves in the wild.

Eimear understood that guests would get frisky while they were away on holiday but what she didn't get was why these particular guests felt the need to leave the evidence littered all around their bedroom. It was as though they were proud of the fact that they were the experienced side of old-aged and were still getting some.

Congratulations guests, Eimear thought, you are old and are getting some. I am young and I am not.

She and Michelle tackled the Sex Pests' bedroom every morning with a vigour that would leave the two from 'How Clean Is Your House' in awe. The number of used condoms she found on bins, around bins or even on the bedroom floor, anywhere but in the bin, astounded her. Initially she naively thought, 'Oh these guests seem like fun! They must have been having water fights!' But after noticing a significant lack of water on the floor, she realised perhaps they were not playing water fights after all.

Lubes and sex toys were left on bedside tables as though they were trophies that deserved awe and admiration. Books giving The Sex Pests hints on what positions they should adopt (should their aging limbs allow them), sometimes with certain pages folded over in the corners to prove their success, were strewn around the room, possibly as an invitation for Eimear to read and take notes.

Eimear did wonder if she would have been so shocked had she not been an individual who had suffered at the hands of Catholic oppression. Regardless of whether her upbringing was to blame for her innocence or not, it had been extremely hard to look The Sex Pests in the eye as she served them beef bourguignon, knowing that the reverse cowboy was their position of choice, that they liked using ribbed condoms or that mint- flavoured tingle lube was a particular favourite of theirs if judging by how quickly they used up the contents of the bottle in just three days.

Admittedly Eimear acknowledged that she needed to see these things in order to forget her frigid education and wake up to the real world where people did have sex. As the season would progress and she would see more evidence of her guests bonking away, she would learn that having sex does not send you to eternal damnation and that probably even God is glad to see his people connect to one another, literally and metaphorically, so well. Eimear decided that He was probably delighted that men and women do at least get some fun out of each other before all the relationship politics gets in the way and picking up the other half's socks becomes the norm. She quickly learnt that condoms were not just for water bomb fights, but used by sensible guests who had been practising safe sex, a good advert to those who think 'sharing (not so nice things) is caring'. She even learnt that STDs were not a band.

However, there were only so many used condoms she could pick up off the floor and by the end of the week of The Sex Pests, she was extremely fed up. She even found herself wishing that her R.E. teacher had been the voice of many people's consciences, something which she had never thought she would long for. But if The Sex Pests had thought that they had to at least try and hide their sexual escapades from God, they might have made more of an effort to hide their sexual litter.

As she cleaned one morning, her phone beeped with the latest plan from Ryan. Even though the text was reminding Eimear that they wouldn't be skiing today as he already had plans with his friends but would definitely be seeing her tomorrow at the top of the ski bubble once she had finished her morning chores, Eimear still flushed in excitement at getting a message from him.

"I honestly don't like him as anything more than a friend!" she exclaimed. Seeing this, Michelle said gently, "Eimear, take it from me. I have so many notches on my bed post, my bed has practically been reduced to splinters. If there is one thing I understand, it is men. He is not just taking you out skiing to be nice. He is doing it because he likes you and I think more than just to try and get in your pants. If he only wanted that from you, he would have tried it on with you in Binky's. Stop being coy, admit you like him and go and have some fun you eejit. That is why you came out here and trust me, if you have the chance to sleep with someone you care about for your first time and he really cares about you, you should do it, no matter the consequences. You never get that first time back."

"Michelle, he is being nice to me because he thinks I am accident prone and feels sorry for me. Honestly, we are nothing more than friends. Come on, let's finish up and head into town. I think it is time I got a new ski kit; although we are just friends, it won't hurt to look sexy while I ski. Um... for you know, the other guys who ski. Not for Ryan, honestly, just for the others..."

With a knowing smile, Michelle finished up the last of her cooking preparation for the night, wiped down the surfaces and grabbed her coat.

It was a good thing she knew her friend so well, Michelle thought to herself. She knew a crush when she saw one and she was going to try her damned hardest to get those two together before the end of the season.

CHAPTER 15

Eimear wasn't sure what her new ski look was going to be but knew she wanted to look cool whilst seductive. Or at least as seductive she possibly could when her face was bright red from concentrating so hard, butt sticking out about a mile behind her in order to maintain her balance because Ryan had once again forced her down a harder slope than last time.

She was determined to not jump on the 'Yo' band wagon, not only because she definitely did not have the moves to pull it off but because she quite liked looking like a girl. She could not understand the female Yos who decked themselves out in the baggiest clothing, making them look like androgynous creatures. However, she also did not want to get anything too tight, other-wise she would look no different from a punter and that was a fate worse than death amongst seasonaire circles. She wanted something just right, something that would ensure she still fitted in amongst the local seasonal workers and maybe something in blue to bring out the colour of her eyes.

In her pre-season life, when she had not lived amongst snow-covered mountain peaks, she had been into her fashion and had, on more than one occasion, to her utter disgust, been referred to as a 'girly girl'. But alas, her behaviour during the ski season did not do much to dispel the reputation. Even though she had been mocked by her friends, Eimear could not help but try to hold on to her femininity. There had been times when she had been so fed up of living in ski gear that she had disregarded her safe, warm, protective snow boots (which she had referred to on more than one occasion unkindly as 'butch shoes') and wandered about the town in her not-so-safe or warm UGGs. She was at her worst when getting ready for a night out on the town; she would utter-ly refuse to wear any of her warm ski gear other than her coat. When she had packed her bags to move out to L'Homme, she had insisted that she could not possibly go anywhere without her party dresses. Even though her mother had pointed out that she would be living in minus temperatures, Eimear had insisted that she would most definitely get use out of them and by God, she had kept to her word. Every Tuesday night, she would lovingly select a beautiful dress to wear, then would don the tights. Oh layers upon layers of the favoured black, nylon material would be pulled on over her particularly unsexy long johns which were rarely removed from her constantly goose-pimpled legs. She may be girly but she wasn't stupid.

Eimear had been appalled when she first moved to L'Homme; her idol, Carrie Bradshaw, would have had a seizure if she had wandered into the ski resort in search of fashion. Not a Jimmy Choo or Manolo Blahnik in sight. But quite quickly, Eimear had realised that high street fashion in L'Homme was an alien concept and the best she could do (Tuesday evenings aside) was embrace the layers and leave her love of fashion behind in Ireland. Over time, Eimear learnt that in L'Homme, cat walks were little paths that had been shovelled out of the snow to allow one's feline household pet to get through the drifts. Labels were something which one wrote dates on and then applied to various covered food parcels in the fridge to comply with health and safety regulations. As Eimear stood in one of the many ski wear shops and flicked through the ski jacket rail, she longed for the sexy sounding labels which filled her fashion magazines at home. She missed names such as Givenchy or Dior, words which belonged to a language that was so beautiful to hear, one could whisper it to themselves all day. The jackets before her eyes had been given masculine brands, words which, when said, sounded as though one had got something stuck in the back of their throat.

These names would have been better suited to places or activities for Action men or G.I. Joes, Eimear thought as she flicked through the latest clothing from Volcom, North Face, Oakley, Bonfire, Spider and Salomon.

But despite her moaning, Eimear was soon filling the changing room cubicles with various ski outfits and by the time the shops were closing for the normal three-hour lunch 'siesta', Eimear was armed with a whole new kit to fall over in and make a fool out of herself on the slopes the following day.

"Fancy going to get a hot chocolate or something?" Eimear

asked, her shopping buzz filling her with satisfied happiness.

"Sounds good," Michelle responded, who was also weighed down with a few bags, "shall we go to La Maison?"

"Oui," Eimear liked to try and throw in the odd French word every now and again to sound like a local.

She really didn't.

She had packed her leaving present from some of her school mates 'Learn French in a few hours!' before leaving Ireland and had boarded her plane with a naive confidence which assured her she would be jabbering away in fluent French in no time. But she had not been as adept at learning the mother tongue of the country she now lived in as she had expected.

Eimear pushed open the La Maison's door and was instantly greeted with the beautiful smell of coffee. The girls wandered over to their favourite window seat and within moments, the usual French waitress arrived by their sides to take their order.

"Un chocolat chaud blanc, s'il vous plait," Eimear said, grinning that she could remember a coherent sentence.

"I will bring it over to you in five minutes." Much to Eimear's disappointment, the waitress still refused to respond in French to her, a sign that her French was still particularly 'merde'.

In her excitement and eagerness to throw herself into French culture, Eimear had forgotten to factor in the many other English-speaking seasonaires, let alone the thousands of British tourists who passed through L'Homme every day. Her need for fluent French was none; although the town maintained its French character and had not succumbed to tacky chains that were found in so many other ski resorts, L'Homme largely depended on its punters to keep its industry alive and so the English language was spoken fluently amongst the French locals.

To hide their incompetence at speaking the language, Eimear and Michelle had launched a vendetta against anyone who would not even try to speak it. As they waited for their hot chocolates, the door swung open and two snow-covered punters sauntered in and made their way to the counter.

"Alright? Two coffees please, ooh and two of those chocolate crêpes too if you don't mind."

The two girls threw a look of disgust in the punter's direction and then turned to one another with a look of superiority. They were seasonaires so that practically made them locals didn't it? And, yes, they may not be fluent in the mother tongue but at least they could say, albeit badly, hot chocolate in French.

But the punters did not stop embarrassing themselves there; one of the duo picked up the lunchtime menu, spotted one of the ingredients and decided to use franglais which would make Del Boy himself envious.

'Alright dar'lin? Mange tout, Mange tout?'

After the embarrassing line rang out through the busy coffee shop, Michelle and Eimear glanced at one another and shook their heads in disdain. What a proud moment for English speakers everywhere. The waitress caught their eye, raised her eyes to heaven and continued to make the various orders in silence behind the counter whilst ignoring the guffaws of the Del-Boy wannabe's friend who thought he was so amusing.

In the brief look the girls had shared with the waitress, they had tried to convey a sympathetic message, one that said that they were sorry for the incompetence of the two men before her and that not everyone for whom English was a first language behaved like that. After all, Eimear and Michelle had said just 'merci' in the best French accent they could muster and did that not surely prove it all?

Underneath this arrogance was a fear that, maybe, someone would discover Michelle and Eimear's deep, dark secret. They were as ignorant as the rest. The few phrases they used were stolen from those who could actually speak French. They would eavesdrop on anyone who could speak the language and write down any phrase that sounded intelligent. But even when the girls gathered the confidence to utter the plundered phrases, they would smile anxiously and silently hope beyond hope that the response would be in English as they didn't stand a chance of understanding anything spoken to them in French.

When the waitress delivered the two hot chocolates made from white chocolate buttons and hot milk, the two girls sank into the deeply-cushioned armchairs and discussed the progress Eimear had been making in the lessons now she was having private ones with Ryan. Michelle was just in the middle of confessing how relieved she was Eimear had been having lessons for she had feared without them, her friend would never have conquered her ski fear when a voice interrupted her.

"I do believe my ears have been burning girls. Are those my ski lessons you are talking about? How'ya?"

Eimear's stomach flipped and she froze in her seat, the shock of seeing him out of context of the ski slopes rendering her silent.

"How'ya Ryan? Here, take my seat, I was just leaving anyway," Michelle said as she downed the last of her hot chocolate.

Jesus Christ almighty, Eimear thought, that girl must have a mouth made of iron to down a hot drink like that. Little git. I know what she is doing.

She shot her friend a warning look but Michelle had gathered her bags up and had left the café with impressive speed before she had even noticed.

"Do you mind?" Ryan asked, gesturing to the chair which still had the shape of Michelle's butt print indented into the cushion.

"Not at all," Eimear responded, finally finding her voice. She took a sip of her drink and racked her mind for something to say.

Goddammit, she thought, normally I never shut up. Words, why have you failed me now?

"Um… you have something on your lip," Ryan pointed to his own lip to show her where to wipe.

That something was a frothy white moustache; she looked like sodding Santa Claus. She swiped her mouth with her sleeve, then realised that using an item of clothing to remove liquid from her face was pretty rank so tried to wipe her sleeve against her jeans leg in an attempt to hide the evident snail trail.

"And you have dribbled a bit there…" again, he pointed to his own jumper as an indication of where she should look.

Eimear glanced down at her jumper and cringed at what she saw. 'Dribbling' was too kind a description for what she had done to her top. 'Flooded' may be more appropriate. In her attempt to hide the mess she had made on her sleeve, she had managed to slop a large amount of liquid down her top. She had been so desperate to hide her messiness from the man she was in awe of, she had not even noticed.

"Oh it is nothing," she said as she surreptitiously dabbed a napkin to her sodden jumper.

Some guys walked into La Maison and glanced over at Eimear. Accidentally catching their eye, she threw them a smile before returning her gaze to Ryan. She was surprised to see he looked a bit annoyed.

"Do you know them?" he asked

"No, just being friendly," she said somewhat perplexed by his question.

"So how are you?" she asked, trying to distract his gaze from the stain on her top and to break the awkward silence after his weird question. "Would you like me to buy you one of those drinks now?" Ryan was refusing to take any money for his time with her on the mountain but had said she could buy him the odd drink every now and again if they bumped into each other.

"No, save it for an alcoholic one next time we are in Binky's. I'm pretty good, even happier to have bumped into you. Well I was only popping in for a second to see if some friends were here but can't see them so had better continue the search. See you tomorrow for the lesson? One o'clock like we agreed? Great, looking forward to it." And with that, he shot her one of his infamous smiles that stretched to his twinkling blue eyes and left the café, leaving a stunned Eimear behind.

Had he really just said he was happy to have seen her and that he was looking forward to their lesson tomorrow?

Something which she had been trying so hard to suppress during all of the other ski lessons when he had been so kind and patient with her, or during the endless analysing chats with Michelle, stirred inside of her as she drained the last of her chocolate. Hope. Forgetting denial for a short while, she finally allowed herself to hope that maybe, just maybe, this beautiful dark-haired, blue-eyed, stubbly Adonis liked her too. Her stomach knotted at the very thought.

But maybe. Just maybe.

CHAPTER 16

The mid-season blues arrived in L'Homme. This infamous grumpy and depressed mood descends on all seasonaires at the beginning of February when the schools across Europe take it in turns to close for half term and children spill onto the slopes. For the whole month, the Alps become infested with families and their kamikaze children, for whom safety and knocking into fellow skiers or boarders like bowling balls is not an issue.

It is during this month that seasonaires tend to do anything other than play on the mountainside in order to avoid the endless queues on the chair lifts or crowding on the slopes. Without the distraction of the magical snow, the Neverland Bubble is momentarily popped and everyone is brought back down to the reality of boring, plain old earth. It is then that the whole seasonaire world realises that they are only half way through the season and therefore still have another two and a half months of pandering to their guests' every whim. Cries of despair and angst echo throughout the ether when every ski resort inhabitant realises they have another ten weeks of rising at stupid o'clock in the morning to cook for moaning guests who still reek of last night's Reblechon and Genepi. When faced with these terrible thoughts, enthusiasm for life is sucked out of even the happiest of souls. Workers can no longer even find it in their hearts to mock the idiosyncrasies of their customers, but choose instead to crawl into their darkened rooms to recover from the season's debauchery so far. There they remain, hidden from the world, until it is safe to emerge from their warm cocoon and the Neverland bubble materialises once again.

This feeling generally lasts until a beautiful, sunny day at the beginning of March when every seasonaire wakes up and notices silence has descended once again in their town. With hopeful eyes, they create a small hole in their curtains, allowing natural daylight into a room which has been deprived of such an honour for the last month. Sleepy eyes peek out of their bedroom window and notice that the footpaths are no longer being monopolised by people who cannot carry their skis properly. At last, their snow-covered peaked playground is free for all to play in. But this glorious day had not yet arrived and Lucy and Ian's team had been suffering quite badly at the hands of the mid-season blues.

Eimear staggered into the living room, head clutched in between her hands with nothing on but her knickers, as had become the normal drunken outfit of choice. She had spent the whole of the night using the toilet seat as a pillow again. As she tried to lift her head into a vertical position from the comfort of her hands, her attention was momentarily diverted from the pain to the sight of the mess that filled every inch of the room. In an attempt to distract themselves from the feeling of melancholy, the team had decided to throw a party in their staff accommodation and had invited all of the friends they had made so far over for a drink or two before heading into town and on to the local club. One or two drinks had, of course, turned into a complete and utter piss-up, replete with Mark's flicking of light switches and more air guitars. The consequence of such a good night was that their home now looked like a scene from Hiroshima, rendering their staff accommodation completely and utterly uninhabitable.

The fridge door had been left open to reveal its contents of curdled milk and mouldy pizza boxes; should Ian and Lucy ever see this vomit-inducing sight, they would quickly question how attentive their staff were to conforming to food hygiene regulations. The sink, which someone had obviously filled in a drunken attempt to clean up before everyone left for town was now a graveyard of crockery and broken glasses, all submerged in greasy, soapless water. The bin looked like a game of reverse Jenga and stank like a morgue on a warm day.

Eimear lowered herself into one of the armchairs, so numb from the hangover that she no longer cared who found her in her semi-naked state, and felt something quite hard underneath her butt cheek. Rooting around under the cushions, quite a daring move, for she feared she may need a tetanus shot afterwards, she found a Bosch drill.

Of course, Eimear thought, such an appropriate place for a drill in the staff accommodation, nestling beneath our cushions.

She gazed around the room in bewildered disgust; burrowed amongst a number of odd ski boots underneath her feet was a deflated blow-up guitar, left over Christmas decorations and unravelled toilet paper someone had chucked around the room after they had tried to dress up as a mummy and failed. Further afield she could see abandoned half eaten plates of food which now housed whole new eco systems. There were broken ski poles, ski gloves, light bulbs, more screw drivers, batteries, a headband, bottle tops, ripped up magazines, screws and a selection of various coloured wigs. Amongst this mayhem, she spotted the array of glasses scattered across the table and the floor which caused her stomach to churn and nausea to bubble in her throat. They still contained various combinations of liquor in them, evidence of the ridiculous drinking games they played the night before.

One of the games was called 'Fives', the aim of which is to guess the correct multiple of five and therefore, escape the drinking punishment.

With each round, all of the players thump their fists three times, a variant of 'Rock, Paper, Scissors' and on the third go, either clench their fist or open their palm. An open palm is worth five, a closed fist is worth nothing. As the fists thump, the person whose go it is shouts out a multiple of five. If, when everyone has chosen either a fist or flat hand, the individual guesses the correct multiple of five, he says 'thank you for a lovely game of fives' without laughing and withdraws his fist, escaping the penalty. If the player guesses the wrong multiple, laughs as he thanks the participants or just withdraws his hand without saying thank you, he will lose his go and the guess moves on to the next player. The ultimate loser is the last person in the game, who is forced to imbibe some evil concoction made by the group.

Eimear's inability to both calculate the five times table and say thank you without laughing explained why she felt as though she would be shaking hands with the grim reaper at any moment.

For every glass Eimear spotted in the room still containing last night's lethal poison, she felt as though they were an insight to and reflection of her transgressions from the night before. She lowered her head into her hands again, partially to hide the debris from her eyes, but mostly to try and block out the flashbacks from the night before. But try as she might, she could not forget the last thing she did before she had run out of Binky's to be sick in the road and ended up being carried home over Rory's shoulder. Oh the shame.

She had been having the time of her life, dancing away on a carefully constructed stage consisting of various sized stools in Binky's when she had toppled off one particularly wonky stool and landed on a Bob. For some reason (in the cold light of sober day, Eimear had absolutely no idea why) she had been particularly enamoured with this Bob. She removed her eyes from the depths of her dark palms and viewed the glasses before her once again, realising that the answer lay before her in the various cocktails of alcoholic drinks she had consumed.

This Bob had seemed charming and funny and, although he still conformed to the Kevin and Perry stereotype, in Eimear's drunken stupor she had decided she didn't care and before long, had stuck her tongue down his throat. After what had been an age of very energetic tonsil tennis, Eimear and her new friend had moved from the dancing area and had monopolised a corner of the bar where things had started to get a little bit frisky. As Slightly-Alright-Bob had started to move his hands down her body, he had leant into her ear and whispered,

"I really want to dick you."

Eimear remembered pulling her head back from the depths of Slightly-Alright-Bob's mouth and had tried to focus on him. When the two men sitting beside her had eventually merged into a single vision and she was able to get a sort of clear look at the man she was snogging, she had assessed the situation. Although the line was possibly the worst one she had heard so far (and she had heard a fair few, the worst until now being Mike Tyson's wannabe's Titanic line) she had been determined to get an interested suitor all night, ever since she had walked into Binky's and had seen Ryan in another dark corner of the bar with his tongue down the village bicycle's throat. All the flirting that had been going on over the last few weeks, the number of times he had gently lifted her up when she had fallen over, the words of encouragement he had given her and the kindness that had laced his praise flashed through her mind as she had stood transfixed, staring at the two of them. Jealousy had flooded through her like fire and she had sworn there and then that she would quash any last hope that lingered in her heart and mind that anything was ever going to happen between them. She had spent the rest of the night ignoring Ryan who had tried a number of times to talk to her and now she had found someone who was actually interested in her. She glanced over to the corner Ryan still occupied with the village bicycle and accidentally caught his eye. He nodded in her direction, and then, checking she was still watching, caressed one of the little slag's butt cheeks and kissed her cheek although not before throwing her Slightly-Alright-Bob a vindictive look. Eimear felt as though someone had kicked her in the stomach. Her gaze returned to Slightly-Alright-Bob and she knew what she had to do. Ok, this was not how she imagined it would happen and maybe it was not the most romantic way to go about it but, if this was the best offer she was going to get, she might as well take it. It would certainly prove to Ryan she didn't care about him.

She had nodded clumsily showing Slightly-Alright-Bob that she was up for it, grabbed his hand and started manoeuvring through the thick crowd of sweaty, heaving bodies on the dance floor towards the exit of the bar. But out of nowhere, a strong, firm hand had landed on her shoulder and was holding her back. At first she had thought it was one of her colleagues checking she was ok but when she realised who it was, she had frantically tried to shrug it off. But no matter how hard she struggled, nothing she did succeeded in loosening the hand's firm grip and eventually, she conceded. Reluctantly, she turned to face its owner.

"You are not going home with him." Ryan's face was close to hers, his voice seething with anger. "He is an absolute scum bag and you should have better taste and sense than that. I am so disappointed with you."

Eimear was shocked.

"Who the hell do you think you are, telling me what to do?" Rage coursed through her veins; first she had to watch him kiss that tramp and now this? As the two of them squared up to one another, Eimear dropped Slightly-Alright-Bob's hand, his presence now completely forgotten. "You aren't my carer Ryan and I certainly am not your responsibility; I don't know why you think you have any authority over me."

Ryan's tone softened and he glanced towards Slightly-Alright-Bob before returning his gaze to the angry girl. "I don't want anything bad to happen to you Eimear, I know that guy. God knows what he carries; he has been with anything that owns a pulse in L'Homme. Please, I am not telling you what to do, I just don't want to see you get hurt or do something you will regret. He is most definitely something to regret!"

"Pot, Kettle, Black Ryan. I can't get with him but it is ok for you to snog the village bicycle? Didn't really see you as a hypocrite but how naïve was I. It isn't a character trait that really suits you; you may want to work on abolishing it for the future. I don't really see why you are so bothered anyway. Run back to your whore of L'Homme and let me get on with my own fun."

Eimear had never felt so angry; she remembered Slightly-Alright-Bob was standing behind her so grabbed his hand and started to push her way through the crowd, dragging him behind her.

But again, the hand with an iron grip reached out and held her back. Eimear lost the plot completely.

"What Ryan? What the fuck do you want?"

"This." And with that one word, Ryan leant down and kissed her.

Eimear went limp; Ryan's strong arms engulfed her to stop her from falling but her mind did not even register, the shock at being kissed by her very own Adonis rendering her weak. The rage that had engulfed her only moments before subsided and, when her lips finally started working again, she kissed Ryan back, hungry for his mouth. Slightly-Alright-Bob gawped at the scene before him, and eventually, aware that he no longer had the hand of the girl he was so sure he would get some from, he did a 360 degree pivot, spotted another likely target and made his way for her without so much as a backwards glance at Eimear. When they eventually came up for air, Ryan whispered into her ear,

"I care because I care for you. And all I want is this." He leant down and lightly brushed his lips against hers. "I only kissed the bicycle because I didn't think you were interested but when I saw you leaving with him... Well I couldn't face it Eimear. I thought it would be better to give kissing you a go and risk being publically humiliated than see you make such a huge mistake with that moron."

In the graveyard that was the morning after the night before, the memory of kissing Ryan still made Eimear's stomach flip. It had been everything she had always imagined it would be and so much more. But then she had gone and ruined it all by being sick into her hand. God, she really hated Jagerbombs, when would she learn? She had run out of Binky's to be sick on the snow-covered road and was closely followed by Ryan who had held her hair back for her and rubbed her back whilst she threw up the content of her stomach. When the vomiting had subsided, he had returned to the bar to find Michelle, who had in turn insisted that Rory, who had been responsible for plying Eimear with the Jagerbombs, carried her home.

As Eimear thought back over last night, she smiled as she remembered the care Ryan had shown her, even when she had disgraced herself. But in the back of her mind, there was a nagging doubt she could not ignore, a doubt that caused her to question whether she had just made a huge mistake. She had kissed someone who had become one of her closest friends, someone who, now she was being honest with herself, she fancied the pants off and surely it could only lead to complications. She knew that seasonaire relationships had their very own best-before dates on them. With only ten weeks to go before the end of the season, Eimear started questioning where kissing Ryan could really go. Could she cope with falling for him when she knew it would definitely end when the seasons changed? But the biggest fear she had, the thought that caused her real trepidation and foreboding was, what if he regretted kissing her when he woke up today? What if he had kissed her just because he was drunk and had decided on a whim that he didn't like seeing her kiss anyone else? Would they be able to return to just being friends if he decided that was all he wanted from her? And if friendship was the only thing he wanted now, could she cope with being nothing more than a friend, now that she had kissed him?

She shook her head to try and escape the thoughts that tortured her, but the movement caused her headache and nausea to increase so she quickly desisted.

Bloody Michelle, Eimear thought angrily, it was all her fault. She was the one who had encouraged Eimear to go skiing with him and she was the one who had continuously left them alone together, giving Eimear time to get to know him better and there-fore, like him more and more. As the reality of how much she liked him dawned upon her, her fear increased as she fathomed how much that kiss could have changed things between them, possibly for the worse. Eimear decided that she was definitely not going to take responsibility for this one even though it was her lips doing the kissing.

But she had a plan. If Ryan decided he wanted nothing more to do with her, she would say that it had been a silly plan of Michelle's, one which Eimear had, in a moment of madness, accidentally succumbed to but she too actually thought it was completely ridiculous and of course she would be fine just being friends.

Maybe if I say it often enough to myself, Eimear thought glumly, I will start to believe it.

As she tried to come to terms with the backup plan and the prospect that Ryan may not ever want to kiss her again, Eimear heard her phone beep in her room. With all the effort she could muster, she threw her legs over the edge of the arm chair onto the only bit of visible carpet left and tiptoed through the debris into her dark cocoon. The outline of Michelle's heavily breathing body was evident beneath the mound of blankets and clothes she had burrowed beneath in her drunken state last night. Anxious to not wake her, Eimear quietly crawled around the floor in the darkness, searching amongst the various piles of crap for her mobile.

She eventually found it under a pile of dirty clothes and clicked open the message. Her heart skipped a beat when she saw it was from Ryan,

I cannot stop thinking about your lips on mine.

I know last night must have seemed like a shock to you but I don't regret it for a second,

I hope you don't either. When can I see you again?

Let's do something other than skiing.

How about we go out for a meal? Are you free tonight? Xx

Eimear stared at the message, not quite believing her eyes. Not only did he appear to not regret the night before, but he was actually asking her out? She re-read the message a number of times before the shock passed and she felt able to come up with a coherent answer.

Fingers shaking, she started typing her response.

Would love to meet up with you tonight.

Are you free at 8?

How about we go to that really cool restaurant in the square? xx

Breath held in excited anticipation, she clicked send and then returned to the arm chair in the living room and stared at her phone, waiting for his response.

Sod it, she thought, throwing all caution to the wind. Wasn't taking risks and stupidly falling for someone what being young was all about? And Ryan was one risk worth taking she decided.

She found a hoodie on the floor, pulled it over her head and curled up in the arm chair. As she clutched her phone tightly in her hand, she rested her weary, sore head on the chair's arm and eagerly waited, her heart pounding from nerves and excitement, for his reply.

CHAPTER 17

It was disgusting. Eimear felt ashamed of herself. She had become one of those giggly girls whom previously she had always detested. She stared at herself in the mirror without really seeing her reflection and, had her mind not been drifting over the events of the last week, she would have seen a sparkly-eyed girl looking back at her with a goofy, lopsided grin plastered across her face. The mere mention of Ryan's name sent her into a dream-like trance. It was enough to make Michelle gag.

"You have gone over to the dark side; I do not envy you for a second." She told the blushing Eimear on a regular occasion whilst poking her deeply in the ribs to try and bring her back to reality.

The last week had spiralled into a whirlwind romance. Eimear and Ryan had met for a meal in the restaurant she had suggested and since then, had not spent a moment outside of work apart. When Eimear wasn't cooking and cleaning and Ryan wasn't showing his guests a new route on the mountain, the two of them would take to the slopes without anyone else and return hours later, flushed from more than just the snow and the skiing. In the evenings, once the two girls had switched the kitchen lights off for the night, Ryan would magically appear outside the chalet with his van and whisk her off into the night.

They had met for their second date the day after their date in the restaurant. After a particularly messy night of cooking, once the kitchen had been cleaned and all the rubbish had been taken out, Eimear waved goodbye to her friends as they drove off without her in the van.

As she watched the brake lights grow smaller in the distance, she tried to suppress the knot that was growing tighter by the second as she thought about Ryan's cryptic clues he had given her about their date earlier that day. All he had said was that she shouldn't get a lift with her colleagues after work, but should dress up warm and wait in the chalet for further instructions.

When she couldn't see the retreating van lights anymore, she locked herself in the downstairs bathroom of the chalet, changed out of her messy cooking clothes and into an outfit carefully selected by the girls earlier on that day. Not that he would get to see it mind as she had been told to dress up in her warmest ski gear and she certainly wasn't willing to undress for him quite yet. It just never hurt to look and feel as sexy as possible. Once she was dressed to impress, she sprayed herself with as much deodorant and perfume as she could feasibly manage without putting her guests at risk of CO_2 poisoning in order to remove the smell of lingering onions from her hair. She then liberally applied enough make up to make her look subtly ravishing and, after a final critical once-over in the mirror, she waited by her mobile in the porch so that she wouldn't be in her guests' way as they settled in front of the TV for the night.

Five minutes stretched to ten, then fifteen and still there was no word from Ryan. As she watched the time drag by on her mobile, every minute without a text felt like an eternity. Just when she started to fear that he had stood her up, she noticed a van turning into the chalet's drive. Knot tightening, she stuck her head out the door and, when she recognised the driver, grabbed her bag and headed out into the cold, dark night.

She opened the van door, pulled herself up onto the passenger seat and they greeted each other awkwardly, smiles awry with nerves. Ryan leant over and gave her a swift kiss on her cheek and then pulled a blindfold out of his trouser pocket.

"Right, don't panic, I am just going to cover your eyes," he said as he leant over to tie the blindfold to her head.

"Uh… excuse me, what the hell do you think you are doing?" Eimear pulled away from his outstretched arms and stared at him dubiously. "That thing is not going anywhere near my head, are you joking?"

"Please Eimear, trust me." She stared at his face and, seeing the desperation for her to play along etched across his face, she shrugged her shoulders and nodded.

But as the van reversed out of the drive, Eimear started to panic. One word entered her mind.

'Kidnap.'

What if she had completely misread his personality and he was not a gentle, kind guy at all but a complete and utter psychopath? What if this blindfold was evidence of a weird and dangerous fetish he had? What if he was taking her away to a hut somewhere in the forest where he would keep her locked up for thirty years? What if, after Ryan was arrested (which, she reassured herself, he would be, everyone knew who she was with tonight) he still refused to give up her location so she would remain hidden until one day, a poor, unsuspecting hill walker stumbled across the snow-covered hut? What would she do for food whilst he rotted in jail? And poor Mr Hill Walker's life would never be the same; after freeing her from her perilous jail, he would be the centre of a media frenzy and constantly hassled by manic paparazzi. How would he cope?

Eimear's imagination ran riot and she started to hyperventilate as the various questions and scenarios flew through her mind with increasing speed. Michelle's raising of the alarm to the police could be too late to save her. Michelle might assume that she had gone back to Ryan's house, by which time she would already be dead and buried in a snowy grave. What if she never got to see her mum and dad again? Or her beloved brothers? Oh God, Michelle was going to find out that it was she who stuck her white jumper in with the red sock and dyed it beyond repair. She wouldn't be around to explain herself and her name would be tarnished forever.

As she panicked over whether Michelle would in fact find the newly dyed pink jumper in its hiding place behind the washing machine or not, she felt the van come to a stop and tiny beads of perspiration broke out on her forehead.

This was it. This was going to be the end for her. Oh God, she really should have done more with her life. And then she realised; she really was going to die a virgin. This truly sucked.

"Wait here, I'll be back in a second," she heard Ryan say, then felt his lips brush against her cheek again.

The touch of his lips on her cheeks sent excited shivers down her spine.

Now that is just weird and sick, she berated herself. You can't find the man who is either about to lock you in a shed or kill you sexy you stupid girl. If I ever get through this ordeal, psychiatrists are going to have an absolute field day with that little reaction. She shook herself in disgust.

She could hear Ryan open the boot of the van and then root around for something, most likely a shovel she concluded. When the back doors shut and she was sure she had been left in the van all alone, she used the opportunity to pull up a corner of the blindfold to sneak a peek at her new environment.

Might as well try and plan an escape route, she thought to herself.

But what she saw was not a cabin in the middle of the woods or a newly dug, open grave waiting for her body. They appeared to be parked on the mountainside and all she could see before darkness engulfed the horizon was the snowy landscape but Ryan was nowhere to be seen.

Perplexed, she dropped the corner of the blindfold and waited for Ryan's return. After what, once again, felt like an eternity, she heard the passenger door open and shivered as the wall of cold air hit her.

"Right, out you get," he said gently, "here, grab my hand and I'll help you down."

Hmm, she thought to herself, seems to be too sweet for someone who is about to kill me.

He carefully lifted her out of the van, put his arm around her waist and led her into the unknown abyss. From the texture under her feet, she could tell she had been taken off the gritted road and, feeling the crunch of compressed snow under her feet, that she was now walking across the mountainside.

After a few more minutes of walking clumsily over the snow, they stopped.

"Right, are you ready?" Ryan asked. Eimear could hear the excitement in his voice.

Images flashes through her mind; the day she received her acceptance letter from her University. Her beloved, smiling family. Her friends at home. The first time she realised she could ski down a whole slope without falling over. Her first kiss although she had to suppress a retch at the last image. Why did she have to think about that one just before she took her last breath? That experience with Rory McGuire had been one she had succeeded in suppressing for a number of years and she was not grateful for her sub-conscious bringing that one up now. She swallowed a sob, took a deep breath and nodded.

Goodbye cruel, cruel world, she thought to herself.

As she felt him remove her blindfold, she scrunched her eyes shut, scared to open them in case what she saw confirmed her worst fears.

"Well open your eyes you eejit."

Slowly, she peeled her eyes open and was not met, as she feared, by a scene out of a horror film. Instead, the sight before her took her breath away. It was the cringiest yet most romantically beautiful thing she had ever seen in her whole life.

Before her was a red, tartan picnic blanket and placed side by side on top of it were two sleeping bags. Beside these was a picnic basket, a wine cooler filled with snow which chilled a bottle of white wine and two wine glasses. On the snow itself, surrounding the whole blanket was a circle of candles, some already extinguished by the slight breeze that blew.

"You aren't going to kill me?" she exclaimed, before clamping her hand over her mouth. She really needed to learn to think before she spoke. "Oh my God Ryan, it is beautiful," she said quickly whilst grabbing his hand and giving it a squeeze, hopeful that this gesture made up for her stupid comment.

Ryan just stared at her, then started to guffaw.

"You really are something else, do you know that? Pick a sleeping bag you moron and grab a glass. The show is going to begin soon. Here, put this on, I don't want you to get cold."

He threw her a woolly hat which she put on without arguing, embarrassed by her outburst. She zipped up her thick ski jacket, clambered into the nearest sleeping bag, grabbed a wine glass as ordered and waited for Ryan to get into his.

"Um… so what am I waiting for? You aren't expecting me to sleep here are you?" she asked, still not quite sure what to make of the picnic sleepover they appeared to be having. She liked the guy, but not so much that she would sleep outside. She had heard rumours that wild boar wandered around the mountainside and wasn't sure if she wanted to stay around long enough to find out if they were true.

"Would you ever shut up for a second," he responded, taking the bottle of wine out of the cooler and pouring her a glass. Putting a small amount into his own, he stretched out his arm, pulled her towards him, and, when she had nestled into his chest, he rested his arm around her and gestured up to the sky.

"Look up."

She tilted her head back to look up at the sky and let out a gasp at the view. It was as though she had bagged front row seats to the uncurtaining of the heavens. The sky was filled with stars and the longer she looked, she realised the sky appeared to be moving.

"Oh my God!" she exclaimed, "there are shooting stars! Look Ryan, look!"

As she glanced over at the man beside her, her stomach gave a jolt as she realised he wasn't looking at the awe-inspiring sight above them, but was looking down at her. His subtle smile and deepening dimples suggested that he was more happy about the date being a success than the view above him.

"It is so unbelievably beautiful, isn't it?" he asked, as he leant over and placed his lips on hers.

When they eventually came up for breath, she slowly sipped on her wine and leant against Ryan's chest and gazed at the view.

She had never felt happier; Ryan kept topping her glass up, neglecting his because he was driving and, when her neck started to ache with looking up at the sky, they had curled up in the sleeping bags and had talked until their mouths were dry.

The date had reluctantly ended when Ryan could feel Eimear starting to shiver with the cold. They had blown out the few remaining lit candles that had survived the breeze, packed everything up and had made their way back to the van.

When Ryan pulled up outside her staff accommodation, he had given another knee-weakening kiss and had asked if he could see her the following day.

And so the week continued like this. They would meet every day and each date ended with promises of a date the following day.

There had been more ski dates, aptly named 'love skis' and they had watched the sunset from another high mountain spot but this time from the warm interior of the van. When Eimear finished work early, there had been late-night dinner dates or drinks in Binky's with all of their friends. Even though they were in public, he had no qualms about placing his arm around her waist or planting a kiss on her cheek, the latter which, for the sake of saving both of their reputations, Eimear tried to discourage after she had caught Michelle miming puking into her hands. In the space of a week, Eimear learnt more about Ryan than she had in the two months before they had started dating.

But the more time they spent together, the more prominent a lingering thought became.

They would probably have sex.

Although this had become her aim for her season, the more of a possibility it became, the more Eimear questioned whether she was really ready to do it. She knew Ryan was fairly experienced in that department, being a hot-blooded male as well as doing so many seasons, and she wondered whether her lack of experience would be a problem.

But alas, the love cocoon Eimear had wrapped herself in could not protect her from the clutches of evil that were Lucy and Ian and it wasn't long before they brought her crashing back down to earth.

CHAPTER 18

The mid-season blues passed as March arrived and everything looked all shiny and new again. With the school term starting, the large family groups went home and the Alps returned to their quieter state. At last, the seasonaires had their playground back.

Michelle and Eimear had just finished their morning work and were standing in the boot room of the chalet getting dressed in their ski gear when Michelle received a call. Seeing the caller I.D., she rolled her eyes and mouthed 'Lucy' to Eimear who grimaced in response as Michelle answered the call.

"Hi Lucy, how are you?" Michelle enquired, her voice dripping with fake sincerity prompting Eimear to let out one of her infamous snorts.

"Um…. No I'm not….." All silky smoothness had gone from Michelle's voice. The change in her tone caused Eimear to look up from the twisted salopettes she had been fighting to get her legs into and she shot her friend a concerned look.

Michelle, seeing that Eimear was watching her, threw her eyes to the ground and turned her back on her friend.

"… Right… oh, ok. Give me a second."

She turned towards Eimear again, covered the mouthpiece and mouthed "Back in a moment". Holding her phone down by her waist, she hurried out of the boot room and through the chalet's front door, shutting it behind her so that she was no longer in Eimear's hearing range.

The euphoria Eimear had felt at the beautiful day and excitement at getting the chance to spend some time with her friend, something she knew she had been guilty of neglecting thanks to her new obsession with Ryan, evaporated. Something was up. Feeling anxious she continued to dress herself, ears pricked waiting for Michelle's return.

Ten minutes later, ski gear on, ski boots successfully strapped on – a challenge she could finally face alone – helmet tied tightly and skis in hand, Eimear sat on the doorstep of the chalet across from hers and waited for her friend. After a short wait their chalet door opened and Michelle, who looked surprised and somewhat guilty to see her.

"Oh sorry," she said, "won't be long" and she hurried into the boot room.

Eimear waited for a few minutes and debated whether she should follow her friend or not. Curiosity won the better of her and leaving her skis and poles resting against the chalet, she entered the boot room.

"What did Lucy want?" she queried, trying to make her voice sound jocular and light-hearted in an attempt to hide her apprehension.

"Oh nothing, just wanted to chat to me about how the season is going." Michelle paused before continuing. "I have to meet her tomorrow for a coffee." She refused to meet Eimear's eye as she said this, but kept her head in the cupboard while pulling on her ski jacket.

"Why does she want to meet you? Does she want to meet me to see how my season is going?"

"I don't know, probably. Or maybe she will want to meet me as a representative for both of us. Anyway," she said hurriedly, withdrawing her head from the safety of the cupboard, "shall we go?"

Eimear nodded and left the boot room to collect her skis. Michelle definitely looked uncomfortable about something but Eimear did not want to push it too far. Her friend was obviously being aloof for a good reason, she told herself. No point badgering her.

But Eimear was aware that she was trying a little too hard to convince herself.

The day passed without the impending meeting being broached again but, although she had a fun day with her friend with much laughter, no matter how much she tried to ignore her instinct, Eimear could not shake the niggling thought that there was more to this meeting than Michelle admitted.

Before the coffee meeting the following day, Michelle was distracted and unusually for her, she continuously made mistakes with the afternoon tea cake. Tired of seeing Michelle's crestfallen face as she pulled out yet another sunken cake from the oven, Eimear took over and shooed Michelle out of the kitchen telling her she may as well leave for the meeting now.

"Better to be early than continuously causing havoc and getting up to no good in the kitchen," she scolded, throwing the failed lump of cake into the bin.

Eimear's kindness made Michelle look more guilty and with an air of awkwardness, her friend left the chalet and made her way into town for her meeting with the much-feared Lucy.

Having successfully made an afternoon cake after just one attempt, Eimear was left to her own devices for the afternoon. She cleaned up the kitchen and joined the remainder of the team who were skiing up the mountain; after a few runs they were joined by Ryan who had spent the morning showing his guests off-piste routes, routes which deviated from the official ski runs. Instead of making sure they had skied down the mountain and returned to the hotel in one piece as he was supposed to, he had abandoned them on the top of the home ski run and skied to the part of the mountain where Eimear and her friends were, to spend the rest of the day with them.

The team could not believe the progress Eimear had made with skiing. Thanks to her one-to-ones with Ryan, she was now a confident skier who looked as though she had been skiing for years instead of months.

Instead of hesitating at the top of runs like she had at the start of the season, she would disappear over the top with speed and poise. She no longer stuck strictly to the run itself but would ski off the edge, finding mounds of snow to leap over. She still looked a bit awkward, she thought, especially if she went a bit too fast for her liking. When this happened, she would throw the back of her skis out and revert to snow plough momentarily until she was happy with the new speed, then would take off down the slope again.

Still, her progress was tangible and she had even tackled red runs, the third most difficult type of run anyone could do in a resort, comfortably. She only had a black run left to do and, while she didn't feel ready to do it yet, she was determined to do one before the end of the season. She couldn't believe how much her attitude had changed towards skiing either. She now absolutely loved it; she felt a real freedom as she whizzed down the slopes, wind in her hair and sunshine on her face. She was even proud that she could overtake some punters! A small win, she admitted, but a sign of progress nonetheless.

While Ryan had been quite a large contributing factor to her development, her team too had helped her by showing patience when she had been stuck at any various points.

She watched Ryan make an effort with her friends as she reflected and her feeling of impending doom was momentarily replaced with smugness. While Ryan taught Leanne how to master the jump she had been having great difficulty with and let Andrew beat him on the race course, she reflected that she was really lucky to have this guy and things were going really well. Mind you, she reflected, it wasn't as though she had all that much to compare it to. She had kissed more than her share of men back at home but had only ever once gone on one proper date and that had been nicknamed 'the date from hell'.

Date-from-hell had been a few years ahead of her at the boys school in her town and they used to flirt every now and again. When he had come home for the summer from his first year training to be a doctor, he had harassed her into submission and she reluctantly agreed to go on a few dates with him. Her disinclination had grown out of a suspicion that, underneath the initial attraction of his profession as a future doctor, he was a complete and utter dud-muffin. She should have trusted her instinct.

On her first date, she discovered he was highly intolerant to drunken behaviour. Admittedly, he did have reason to complain; he had seen her at a house party the night before where she had not been on her best behaviour. True to tradition, she had stripped off in order to hug her favourite object – the toilet – when highly intoxicated and when she had eventually wandered away from her porcelain pillow (luckily remembering to dress herself before she did), she had fallen asleep in the laundry cupboard. Surprisingly, although he had seen her in this state, he had still arranged to meet up with her the following day so she had assumed it had not bothered him all that much.

Oh how wrong could one be; not only did he lecture her on the dangers of drinking but he proceeded to ask her if she felt 'sheepish' for her behaviour, did she have anything to say for herself and was she going to behave that way again in the future.

Prick.

Yet for some unknown reason, she agreed to a second date with him. It wasn't as though the signs hadn't been there or that she was naïve enough to believe he would have a personality transplant before they met up again. Hindsight really was a bitch but she had no one to blame but herself.

If she had thought the first date bad, Date-from-hell really outshone himself on the second date. It had started off fairly well in that he did not start lecturing her the moment he saw her. But within half an hour, it had plummeted to rock bottom; he began insulting her family, in particular her two older brothers who he had played on a hurling team with. Then he had started criticising her personality, saying that he knew she had a reputation for being a little bit on the 'attitude' side and that her proper place should be one of 'being seen and not heard'. Finally, he had told her that her mother should not have developed a career for herself but stayed at home. After all, the only place for a woman was in the kitchen but that was only when she wasn't pushing out as many babies as possible. With each line, Eimear became a little bit more incredulous. Was this really happening or was she going mad? Maybe her sanity was safe and she was just having a bad dream? A quick, hard pinch to her inner thigh confirmed her fear; she was not in a nightmare so was either going mad and imagining this whole façade or, much, much worse, this conversation was actually happening. The real corker that ensured she would never, ever go on a date with him again came after they had been handed their main course and had been wished 'bon appetit' by the waiter.

"So Eimear. When are we, you know," his eyebrows bobbed up and down in some sort of suggestive manner. When it was met with a blank face, he continued, "You know, have sex.

Because to be honest, I am getting bored just dating you."

Eimear had choked on her spaghetti bolognaise. Never in all of her life had she been so horrified; she would have chosen repeating her mother's crime-worthy sex education lesson over spending another second with this moron any day. The date had continued in mortified silence (on her part) and an egotistical monologue (on his).

After he had paid the bill (she had begged to pay half just in case he thought she now owed him something but her pleas had been silenced with "I wouldn't be much of a gentleman if I accepted". Gentleman my arse, she had thought) he had made a crude attempt to fondle her tiny excuses for breasts whilst helping her put on her coat.

She could not get out of that date quickly enough.

God bless his patients in the future, she had thought after the second date, especially if any of them liked a bit of a drink or was a working mother.

Even though that was the only dating experience she had so did not have much to compare her current relationship with, she did feel as though she was lucky with Ryan. Every now and then, when he was in the middle of doing something for one of her friends, he would catch her eye and send her a smile that made her feel as though she was the only girl in his world. She would, admittedly, feel embarrassed and slightly nauseous that she could be that smitten and lame; she would look around her quickly to make sure no one else witnessed her blush-induced rosy cheeks.

Spending the day with her friends and Ryan helped her shake off the weird feeling but once she returned to the staff accommodation, the nerves came flooding back. Walking into her room, she saw Michelle was lying on top of her bed listening to music through her headphones. The moment she saw the look on her friend's face she knew everything was not ok. Her eyes were tightly scrunched up and she looked pale, her forehead was lined with wrinkles and her hands, which were resting on her stomach, were tightly knotted. Her foot was the real indication that something was wrong; Michelle was tapping it against the bedpost with such vigour, Eimear feared the bed would disintegrate under the force.

She watched her friend for a second, unsure whether she should disturb her but curiosity and concern got the better of her. She sat on the edge of Michelle's bed and her friend's eyes flew open in alarm, her body jumping slightly as they did so. Realising who it was, Michelle pulled out her headphones, smiled at her friend and sat up, curling her legs underneath her as she did.

"Hey you, how was the mountain?" she asked brightly, obviously faking enthusiasm in her attempt to make an effort at appearing normal.

"Really good, you should have joined us."

Michelle nodded but didn't say anything; as she stared at a spot on the wall, she began twisting her fingers together in a knot once again.

"So what did Lucy want?" Eimear asked after the silence became unbearable. She felt far too uncomfortable; she had never felt awkward around Michelle before, it was not a situation she knew how to handle well.

"Oh you know, just wanted a general chat really about the season, how it was going and were we happy. That sort of rubbish really."

Michelle still stared at the invisible spot on the wall as she spoke, as though she was in some sort of trance and could not bring herself to look into Eimear's eyes.

"I think I am going to have a shower," she said suddenly snapping out of her reverie, "do you know if anyone else is using it?"

Eimear shook her head; Michelle glanced over at her, nodded and swung her legs over the side of the bed, carefully avoiding her friend as she did.

"Right so, back in a minute." She grabbed her towels and walked out of the bedroom, her shoulders hunched and her head hanging low as she did.

Eimear watched her retreating back in confusion; there was nothing they could not or had not discussed, no trouble they had not shared or an incident that they had not worked out a solution to. So why was her supposedly best friend being so secretive?

When she finally accepted there was nothing she could do to explain her friend's behaviour, she looked around at her room that had, once again, deteriorated into a bomb site and decided to spend a few minutes sorting everything out before she too had a shower.

She started by picking up the pile of clothes next to the bed which belonged to Michelle and, as she folded them into piles, a letter dropped out of the back pocket of a pair of Michelle's jeans. Not paying much attention to it, she bent down to pick it up but as she placed it on the shelf where Michelle kept her notepads and books, she noticed that her name had been handwritten across the top of it in Lucy's writing, followed by a question mark. Although she knew to look would be a violation of her friend's privacy, curiosity once again got the better of her and she decided she had to know why. She stuck her head out of the bedroom door to check that the shower was still running and, satisfied that Michelle would not be back any time soon, she closed the bedroom door, sat on her bed and unfolded the piece of paper.

What she saw made her blood run cold. White noise filled her head and as much as she tried, no, needed to, she could not tear her eyes away from the incriminating ink-stained letter before her.

A noise finally made her look away and standing in the middle of the doorway, towel wrapped around her midriff and hair dripping water all over the floor, was Michelle.

The white noise was quickly replaced by rage.

"Yours I believe," Eimear hissed as she balled the piece of paper up in her hand and chucked it at her friend. It landed at Michelle's feet and when she realised what Eimear had thrown at her, the colour drained from her face.

"Where did you get that? Did you read it?" her voice was barely audible.

"Yeah I did. What the fuck Michelle?" Eimear's voice was laced with fury and her hands were shaking. She glared at the now slumped girl in the doorway who was staring at her feet and shifting from side to side, her discomfort oozing out of every pore.

"Well? I am waiting for an answer from you. What, in the name of Jesus, is this all about?"

121

Biding her time, Michelle bent over, picked up the offending piece of paper and timidly crept towards Eimear. When Eimear didn't state any objections to being so close to her, Michelle sat down on the bed.

"I didn't know how to tell you Emsie, I am so so sorry. As you can see from the letter, there have been complaints. Well, lots of complaints actually…. Some about me but to be honest, most of them have been about you. That is what the phone call was about yesterday. Lucy received that letter from guests we had a few weeks ago and wanted me to meet her today to tell her… to tell her…"

Her voice trailed off and she swallowed nervously as she calculated the best way to say what she had to say next.

She took a deep breath and continued, "…to tell her whether there was cause for concern and if you had in fact done the things the guests had accused you of."

Silence descended in the room. Eimear could not believe what she was hearing. She racked her brains and thought about the events over the last few months to see if there was anything particularly bad she had done to warrant such complaints.

Unable to think of anything completely atrocious, she spluttered,

"But that letter just complains about the fact that I burnt the food. What else have guests said I have done?"

"Some complained that you didn't clean the taps properly and she knew that you sometimes wear your pyjamas to work in the morning, that you have cooked with your hood up… the guests guessed that you were hungover… and they told Lucy."

Heat rushed to Eimear's cheeks. Admittedly, she had burnt quite a few dishes and it was not uncommon for her to turn up to work in her pjs and a hoodie, especially if she had had a late one the night before. But the tap? Complaints about water marks on a bloody tap? For God sake!

She addressed this last thought quite vocally, introducing a string of expletives in all the relevant places to Michelle who nodded miserably.

"And why didn't you tell me that was what the dragon wanted

to speak to you about? Why didn't she just speak to me?"

Michelle shook her head and then shrugged, "She thought you would try to deny it and I didn't want to tell you because I knew you would be hurt and upset. I am so, so sorry Eimear, I really, really am."

Eimear's voice lost its anger but was replaced with quiet disbelief as she asked her next questions. "Did you tell her that the guests' feedback was actually true?"

Michelle accidentally caught Eimear's eye, lowered her head quickly and then reluctantly nodded.

Betrayal seared through Eimear's body, leaving her breathless. She could not believe her friend would deceive her this way and she stared at her blankly.

"I am so sorry Eimear," Michelle repeated, "I told her I had done some things too, honestly I did. But she just wanted to focus on your complaints. I really tried to stick up for you, really."

Eimear had heard enough. She wanted to get away from this stuttering Judas before her, away from the disgust she felt, away from the person who had kept something so serious from her and away from the hurt she felt which continued to grow the more she realised her friend had sold her out to her boss. But most of all, she wanted to escape from the fear she felt, a fear that arrived when she realised that these complaints could cause her to lose her job and return home before the end of the season.

Not wanting to hear Michelle's verbal diarrhoea of excuses any longer, she grabbed her ski coat and started to walk out of the room.

"Where are you going?" Michelle asked

"Out."

"Will you be back in time for work?"

"Don't know but I am sure you will manage just fine without me since you are so goddam perfect and I am nothing but a walking liability!"

And with that, Eimear slammed the bedroom door and stormed out of the staff accommodation into the darkening night.

CHAPTER 19

Eimear didn't know what to do so wandered aimlessly through the streets of L'Homme; she had never felt so alone. When she had any problems previously in the season, Michelle had been the one she had spoken to about it. Now that Michelle was the problem, there was only one other person she could think of who would make it ok. She fished her phone out from her pocket and scrolled though her recent contacts until she found the number she had been looking for.

"Hello petal, how are you?" The moment she heard her mum's voice answer the phone, she felt some of the weight shift from her shoulders.

The emotion and confusion Eimear had felt bubbled to the surface and for ten minutes she poured her woes down the phone to her mother, only pausing to take the occasional gulp or release an emotional sob and nasal snort.

"What awful gobshites," her mother hissed the moment Eimear finished telling her story. So shocked was she at hearing her mum utter a swear word, her sobs momentarily ceased. "I mean, really. They call themselves professionals? Adults? Ooh I would love to call them up and give them a piece of my mind."

Eimear was stunned. Never, in all her eighteen years of existence, had her mother ever criticised someone who was in a position of authority. If she or her brothers had ever received a detention at school, it was the norm for her mum to call the teachers up, not only to apologise for the child-in-question's behaviour but to enquire as to whether there was any further punishment she could deal out at home. For her mother to condemn an employer... well, hell must have frozen over. Either that or one of the boys had left his sports gear lying around the house and Eimear had just provided the ample excuse to release her frustrations.

"Mama, what should I do? I don't want to go and work with Michelle tonight, I am so angry with her. She should have told me but instead she stabbed me in the back and arse-kissed Lucy."

"Jesus Eimear, you really are getting rough around the edges.

Mind your language please young lady, or I will be getting you etiquette lessons for your birthday."

Eimear raised her eyes to heaven and contemplated pointing out her mother's previous (and far worse) swearing but, knowing from past experience it was pointless to argue with a woman who claimed she was always right, she decided against it. She also remembered that she was fighting with enough people and would prefer to avoid her mother's sharp tongue which would undeniably surface should Eimear challenge her use of certain words.

"You need to go back home and speak to Michelle. I know she hasn't behaved appropriately but try to see things from her point of view. Her eejit of an employer summoned her and put her in an extremely awkward position. I doubt that she didn't tell you for malicious reasons petal, I am sure she only did it to protect your feelings. Now I am not saying what she did was right..." her mother's voice rose over the sound of Eimear's stuttering protests, "but I am merely telling you to calm down for a moment and get some perspective."

Eimear stomped her feet and rolled her eyes; she was always telling her to 'calm down and get some perspective.' She was calm for Christ sake! She thought she had not acted dramatically at all, but had been very well behaved giving the circumstances. Admittedly, she could have not stormed out of their home... or slammed the door... but Jesus! It was not like she had dramatic tendencies or anything, she simply embellished her emotions sometimes. Coincidentally, her histrionics just happened to emerge around the same time some incident had occurred.

"As for those moron bosses of yours, I think you should speak to them. If they have issues with you and your work ethic, it is you they should be talking to and not Michelle. Arrange a meeting with them and ask to go through the complaints that have been made, they need to hear your side of the story. Mind you pet, you are a pretty awful cook, I mean, look what you did to our kitchen and that was when you were just cooking bacon so maybe they have a point."

"Mum, I only burnt the kitchen once and that was an accident, you know I didn't mean to leave the grill on whilst in the shower. Will you ever let that drop? And I have got better since then, honestly."

"Now that is the arsey little daughter I know and love. Get some of that fire back in you and go and make up with your friend. There is not long left in the season and you don't want to spend what is left of it fighting with one of your oldest and closest friends over two incorrigible fools like Lucy and Ian, they really are not worth that."

"Incorr-what?"

"Incorrigible, Eimear, incorrigible! For God sake girl, and you want to do English at university? Buy yourself a dictionary! Listen petal, I have got to go. Your brother has just come in from hurling and has dropped his gear all over the floor which has just added to the pile of rugby gear your father has left all over the kitchen. It looks like a pitch-worth of mud has been dragged in and I need to hunt them both down and give them a bollocking."

Again, Eimear's heart stopped. 'Gobshites', 'arsey' and 'bollocking' all in the same conversation? She held the phone away from her ear for a few seconds whilst checking the caller I.D. to make sure it definitely was her mother she had called and not some imposter who, up to that moment, had been doing an amazing job of imitating her.

They said their goodbyes; her mother's words always had a calming effect on Eimear but now she found herself longing for the normality of her home life. She missed the small things, even the mess her brothers and father made and, although she would never admit it, her mother nagging them until they were ready to burn their ears off just to get rid of the sound of her voice. Sighing, she thought over her mother's advice. She knew she was right and that she should go home to Michelle but she could not bring herself to face her friend and make amends quite yet.

She decided to take the long way home which should get her there with enough time to get ready for work. The walk would do her good and clear her head, giving her the little 'bit of perspective' her family were always encouraging her to obtain.

En-route, she saw a little grotto on the side of the road. She had noticed it before when the van had trundled past when going to and from work but she had never had the chance to investigate it closely.

She stepped onto the snowy verge and, pushing herself onto her tiptoes, peered through the bars into the cavern. When she saw what was inside, the feeling of homesickness she had experienced but successfully suppressed only moments before exploded, leaving her feeling as though she had an empty hole in her stomach.

Within the chamber stood a statue of a praying Virgin Mary surrounded by fake lilies. Inscribed on the walls behind the statue was something in French, a prayer Eimear assumed, and tied to the bars of the grotto were tiny bouquets of now wilted flowers with tiny messages scribbled on them. Although a bizarre scene to anyone who was not familiar to such icons, seeing the grotto brought a feeling of nostalgia to Eimear. Scattered across the roadsides throughout the Irish countryside, larger-than-life statues were erected, portraying various Biblical scenes. Her grandparent's generation still made the sign of the cross as they passed them, something Eimear's generation had rebuked to maintain their 'cool' image. Now, she longed to watch the elderly show reverence to a religion they so strongly believed in. It was odd that symbols that had bugged her so much both at home and on arrival in France were the things that gave her so much comfort now. She gazed upon the statue before her and laughed softly at the irony of finding solace in the very thing she had been fleeing from.

This really was a bemusing situation, Eimear reflected. Of all of the countries she had run away to, it was one where Catholicism was as prominent as it was in Ireland. How could she think somewhat inappropriate, dirty, sexual thoughts in guilt-free peace with miniature statues of the Virgin Mary scattered across the place? God really was omnipotent, there really was no escape.

"You can hide from me but you can't hide from God," her teacher's famous line echoed through her brain once again.

Do one Miss! Eimear thought, although with a hint of a nostalgic smile and far less hostility than she would have mustered had her conscience piped up months before.

With a final look through the bars, she smiled again and turned away to continue her journey home.

Her raunchy, sexual thoughts had become more frequent as she had spent more time with Ryan. They had 'done stuff' and had she stayed at his house longer when these deeds were taking place it would have been highly likely that they would have ended up 'doing it.' But something always stopped them, usually a frantic phone call from Michelle telling her that she had to get her backside home to shower, change and get ready for their evening shift at work.

Eimear's thoughts had recently been dominated by sex; she assumed it was because having it was becoming more of a possibility and she felt a slight fear of the unknown. Whatever the reason, she could not stop pondering about what sex would be like and, more specifically, what it would be like with Ryan. Sex had been discussed in quite some detail between the two of them, something Ryan had insisted on when he had discovered Eimear was still a virgin.

She had been nervous about telling him, as though discovering she was not 'de-flowered' would in any way change his opinion of her. She had never really opened up to anyone about something so intimate before and she was surprised at how raw and vulnerable she had felt about sharing details of something so personal to her.

After telling him, she had waited in the silence that had filled the room for his verdict, waited for his condemning words that were sure to follow. With a heavily-beating heart, she had stared at a spot on his clothing-filled floor, too scared to look at him. But his reaction had been quite contrary to her expectations. He had lowered his face to meet hers, stroked her hair, kissed the end of her nose and then released the largest grin she had ever seen.

"Yes!" he had exclaimed almost triumphantly, "I am so glad! I will go where no man has gone before!"

She had looked at him somewhat disgustedly. What the hell was he on?

"Ryan, that is gross and completely inappropriate. Plus don't get too cocky or assume you will be the one I sleep with, talk about a turn off."

"Yeah, whatever," he grinned. "Sorry, ignore me. We will just take it slowly ok? There is no rush," he had said, then gave her another deep, hard kiss before Michelle the Time Keeper had phoned and Eimear had to rush back to get ready for work.

Still feeling upset and a little bit homesick, she decided to call Ryan on the remainder of her walk home, thinking that hearing another Irish accent would do her some good.

"How's it going?" his chirpy, lyrical voice answered the phone immediately.

"Grand, yourself?"

She almost wished she hadn't asked; the moment the question left her lips, Ryan boarded the Tangent Express and, in excited flurried chatter, he told her all about the exciting route he had planned for his guests the following day, that more snow fall was expected over the following weeks and that he was going to get so drunk on his night off, he would probably wet his bed.

Remember not to stay over on that night, Eimear told herself.

"That's great," she said, the moment she could get a word in, "but something happened today that I was hoping to talk to you about and maybe get some advice from you?"

She started explaining her Michelle and Lucy dilemma, feeling herself getting upset as she did but Ryan cut in half way through her story.

"Oh dear, that sounds bad," he said, a little bit disingenuously, "Listen Eimear, I have got to go but I will call you later ok? Maybe you can come over after work and we will watch a DVD? It might cheer you up a bit; I will call you later with the details ok? Right, bye."

And with that, he was gone.

Eimear removed her phone from her ear and stared at her screen dumbstruck. He had never ended a conversation like that with her before. Feeling slightly snubbed and disgruntled, she put her phone back in her pocket and, seeing her home in sight, dragged her weary, reluctant feet towards her front door.

Maybe he really did have to go, she told herself, seeking any excuse she could to explain his behaviour. But she did not have time to worry about his bizarre departure for long; taking a deep breath, she climbed the steps, opened the front door and stepped into the staff accommodation.

It was time to face the music with Michelle.

CHAPTER 20

Eimear had accepted, although she would never openly admit it, that her mother was right. She knew it would be the best thing for her and for the sake of the rest of her season, to make amends with her friend. She had been completely prepared to do so by the time she had walked through The Palace door but the moment she had laid eyes on Michelle's nervous, guilty face, she had felt her anger re-emerge.

Flicking your ex-friend in the face is possibly not good grounds on which to re-establish your friendship, Eimear had to remind herself as she resisted the urge.

Dinner service was strained that night. As they chopped, sautéed and fried, the tension between them was palpable but through gritted teeth and strained smiles, they attempted jokes and friendly conversation for the benefit of their guests.

After they had tidied away the last of the dessert plates, Michelle cleared her throat in an attempt to get her friend's attention and asked cautiously,

"Do you want to do something tonight? Watch a film? Go for a drink?"

Eimear didn't look up from the soapy quagmire she was scrubbing dishes in, a task she found unusually engrossing, as she responded in broken English,

"Can't. Watching DVD. At Ryan's."

A gasp from Michelle momentarily distracted Eimear from the dark depths of her soapy refuge and to her ex-friend's shocked faced instead.

"What," she snapped at her. She was in no mood for any of Michelle's histrionics.

"You are going to have sex!" Michelle exclaimed, forgetting to lower her voice in front of the guests who were lounging in the snug nearby.

"Shut up fool, they can hear you! And what in the name of God are you talking about? I am watching a DVD with him, I just told you. Nowhere in that statement did I say I was having sex."

Michelle shook her head and timidly moved closer to her friend, as though afraid to bridge the gap with the girl who still had anger oozing out of every pore.

"It is a code," she whispered, finally aware that the guests were still in their presence. "When a guy asks you over to watch a DVD, it really means he wants to have sex with you."

Eimear stared at her friend in silence for a couple of seconds, washing-up liquid dripping from her yellow rubber gloves.

"You have completely lost the plot," she said dismissively, turning her back on Michelle and continuing with the washing up. "I am going over to watch a DVD and nothing more."

The girls returned to cleaning the kitchen in silence for the remainder of their shift and did not resume conversation once they returned to The Palace. She knew it was petty, but even in the rare moments when her anger subsided, she could not think of a way of broaching the tension and ending the animosity. Accepting that she and her friend would not resolve their issues that night, she hopped into the shower and then swept through the room, packing an overnight bag without saying a word. There had been a brief instant where she considered asking for some advice on what to take, having never stayed over at a guy's house before, but stubbornness won and she came to a clothing conclusion on her own.

As she headed out of their bedroom door, Michelle meekly piped up,

"Look. I know you don't want to speak to me and I understand why but how about I pick you up in the morning before work? It will save you walking into town to get the bus. Say 7.30?"

Eimear was going to snub the offer but getting a lift allowed her at least an extra half an hour in bed…. Why be childish?

"Ok, um… Thanks. I will be ready and waiting outside."

"Ok. And Eimear? I know you think nothing will happen tonight but just in case, be careful and… good luck."

Eimear shot her a bemused look; what was this obsession with DVD-related sex? Too confused to comment she merely nodded her head and headed out the door into the cold, dark night.

Oh how she hated it when she was wrong; thank God she had

had the self-awareness to shave all of the necessary places.

On arrival at Ryan's house, she had been welcomed into his newly tidied room and was invited to take a seat on his bed whilst he organised the DVD. As the disc loaded, he sat beside her and engulfed her in a bear hug which, as well as pressing her into his rock-hard chest, coincidentally enabled him to flex his bulging biceps. When she freed her face from his unnecessarily preened armpits, she gasped for some much needed air and attempted to broach the subject of Michelle but he lunged for her mouth and started kissing her. Initially, she was reluctant to reciprocate as she suspected the kissing was more to do with shutting her up than a feeling of overwhelming desire for her. After a few minutes, however, she no longer cared about his intentions and found herself kissing back enthusiastically. The menu music started booming through the room so Ryan untangled himself from her grip, pressed play and leapt over to the other side of the room where he punched the light switch. As the room was plunged into darkness with only the laptop for light, he dived back into the bed in one smooth move and snuggled into her once again.

He seemed particularly energetic tonight, Eimear had observed. He was not too dissimilar from a child who knew his birthday was approaching and could not contain himself for all the excitement he felt.

Little did she know.

What had started out as innocent snuggling at the beginning of 'The Notebook' (his choice, not hers) had quickly progressed to some heavy petting in various stages of undress. As her t-shirt was peeled off, alarm bells started to ring. Her underwear and bra were not matching! Alarm bells progressed to foghorns as she started internally debating matching-underwear politics. Should your bra and underwear always match? Did guys even notice these things? Why hadn't she just matched and played it safe? And why oh why was she such a tramp and not done laundry for a while? She tried to glance down at the undergarments she had selected and cringed at what she saw. The items now on show for Ryan had been the only two clean undergarments she owned. What were possibly once white, gleaming bra and knickers were now a gruesome shade of yellow.

Eimear attempted to surreptitiously cover herself with his duvet but her attempt was quickly aborted when Ryan made a grab for her chest. He appeared to be more interested in removing the offending items than observing the discoloured bra and the slightly granny-esque pants she had on, so Eimear decided that she could only assume it was not the priority on a man's copulating preference list.

Jesus Eimear, you do worry about the most ridiculous things at the most inconvenient times, she scolded herself as she threw her attention back onto the man beside her.

One thing became quickly apparent; Ryan's enthusiasm for the night was somewhat inspired by his apparent confidence that they were going to 'do it'.

As this realisation slowly dawned upon Eimear, she was filled with complete and utter terror. Was she really about to lose the very thing that she had placed on a pedestal for so many years, the thing she had given so much thought and value to?

Questions ran through her mind. Was she definitely sure she wanted to? Here? Now? With him? She glanced down at Ryan who had somehow managed to lose all clothing bar his boxers and – oh Jesus Christ – his bloody socks. When had he managed to remove his other items of clothing? And what, in the name of all that was good in the world, had possessed him to keep his socks on? Had he, at some point in his life, wandered past a mirror when he had only dressed himself in those toe-warming items, and decided it was a good look for him? That it would make him a sexy, irresistible beast to women? Because if so, someone needed to tell him he was most certainly wrong. They weren't even matching; on his left foot, he had a grey sock with holes in and on his right, he had an orange sock.

As Eimear started to turn her nose up, she remembered her non-matching dilemma and quickly rethought her position on the sock front. He who cast the first stone and all that. Now may not be the right time to be quoting biblical references she quickly reminded herself. Also, telling herself to not be judgemental did not cause much comfort as he still looked like a complete and utter tit.

Ryan started kissing the side of her neck and as his hand wandered, she could feel her body stiffen up slightly. In return for each kiss he placed on her skin, she awkwardly pecked at any available piece of skin.

This was something she had wanted to happen, she reminded herself, something she decided she wanted before she had moved to France. But escaping the grasps of Catholicism was not as simple as she had imagined. Firstly, there were all those bloody grottos scattered around L'Homme as well as the odd austere crucifix peering down on the crowds as they scurried around the town.

It was enough to make anyone feel self-conscious; a semi snow-submerged naked Jesus hanging on his cross, observing your every move about the town would be enough to make even the most devout atheist feel self-conscious.

But secondly, and possibly most dangerously, Catholic guilt was something that was carried in her psyche. This was far harder to escape.

Yes she was scared of the act of sex itself but far more terrifying for her was the fear that she would regret it and gargantuan remorse would be sure to follow. She feared that she would wake up tomorrow in the arms of someone she had only known for a matter of weeks, albeit intense weeks, in a bed that was not her own and regret giving up something of such importance. She could never get her virginity back and what was more, whatever happened with Ryan, he would always be a memory she would have with her for the rest of her life. She knew that one's first time would never be forgotten. What if this person who she gave herself to tainted the memory forever because he ended up being a massive jackass?

Oh sod it, she thought, as her body relaxed with each kiss.

Ryan's kissing got more frenetic and she had to admit that this felt quite good. She started to relax and reflected that although she had not known Ryan that long, she felt like she had known him all of her life as she had spent so much time with him. He was also caring, sweet, sensitive and, not that it should matter, so goddam fit.

Ryan levelled his face with hers and whispered, "Do you want to?", then suggestively lurched his head in the direction of her crotch and wiggled his eyebrows up and down, a move which Eimear assumed meant 'have sex.'

Did she want to?

Despite the fear, anxiety and nerves that possessed her body, there was one emotion creeping to the forefront, overriding everything else.

Curiosity.

As last, this was her chance to find out what the big deal was, what someone's sex face really looked like and, most important-ly, find out what the hell 'the wheelbarrow' actually was.

She had promised herself adventure and change on her ski sea-son and, now that she finally had that opportunity, she would not let herself down.

Before another thought could enter her mind and possibly sway her decision, she nodded quickly.

Like a child who had just been told they had received a year's worth of candy floss, Ryan's face lit up. With frenzied move-ments he started rooting around in a drawer beside his bed and fished out a small square foil packet which reminded Eimear of her water bomb days at school. A small, nostalgic part of her wished she could be there now and, supressing a small smirk, she contemplated whether Ryan would appreciate her suggestion of forgetting the sex and having a water bomb fight instead?

Probably not.

As she watched him roll it on, an action which she found to be anything but erotic as it reminded her of the skin on sausages, she considered how gross the build-up to sex was. Without warn-ing, she was horrified to hear the lecturing voice of her mother boom through her mind.

"An erect penis has no conscience."

Eimear rolled her eyes and tried to bury her head into the back of the pillow in an attempt to drown out the sound of her mum's voice.

Mum, I swear to God, Eimear told herself, now is not the time to make your way into my consciousness!

Ryan finished rolling the weird sausage skinned-shaped thing on and Eimear was relieved to discover that her mother's voice had disappeared. But the feeling was short lived as panic started to rise as this turgid thing loomed before her in the semi-darkness of the laptop-lit room. For the second time in the matter of minutes, another solitary warning arrived in her already semi-guilt ridden mind.

"You can buy second-hand clothes but no one will want a second-hand woman"

The voice of her R.E. teacher had arrived and was reciting one of her favourite lines from her lessons at school. For God sake, Eimear's head screamed. Right, that is it! No more penis warnings and no more 'used women' analogies! I am doing this and that is that. Final!

This rant was met with silence. Conscience quietened, Eimear started querying what she was supposed to do during the act of sex. She remembered once overhearing her mother one Christmas discuss sex with her aunts when they were all in a particularly inebriated state. As they sniggered over their umpteenth glass of wine, empty bottles scattered around them, one of the sisters squawked,

"I just lie back and think of Ireland!"

All the sisters collapsed in fits of giggles, hiccupping and snorting into their glasses as they did.

And as Eimear lost her virginity in the snow-filled winter wonderland of L'Homme, that is exactly what she did too.

CHAPTER 21

Eimear lay in the nook of Ryan's arm, curled up as tightly as possible so both of them could fit into his tiny, single bed. She listened to his deep, heavy breathing as he slept beside her. She couldn't sleep; she was waiting for the barrage of emotions, mainly guilt, to hit her but it never came. Instead, other feelings materialised; elation that she had actually had sex, excitement that she too could finally talk about positions with some sort of (albeit it, minimal) knowledge but mostly, the main feeling that dominated her psyche was perplexity.

Was that it?

If that was all sex was, she really didn't see what the fuss was all about. Ok so it felt good at the time and she had enjoyed herself, but if that was all it was ever going to be, she would prefer a cup of tea and a good book.

As Ryan let out a loud snore, Eimear felt a little bit bad that she was being slightly critical, especially when she had nothing to compare it to and as Ryan had been so attentive and caring to her when it was over. He had continually asked her if she was ok, if she was in any pain and if she was glad it happened. And she was glad; she had not felt any regret, just a little bit self-conscious as she lay exposed to this slightly older and much more experienced man.

But if she had held any doubts or regret, Ryan's news which he had broken to her post-coitus would have chased them away immediately.

As he held her close, spooning her into his chest, he had whispered in to her ear, "There is something I have to tell you."

Initially she had feared the worst. The condom had broken and she was pregnant. The condom had broken and she had syphilis. The condom had broken, she was both pregnant and had syphilis and, now that he had had his sexual fill, he was ending it.

But it was none of those.

"I am returning to Ireland at the end of the season and am getting a job in Dublin. I think it is time I joined the real world again so I was wondering, if you were interested, whether you would like to carry this on when you get home?"

Eimear had said nothing at first, so surprised and happy was she to hear this thing that they were going through no longer had an end date. But he misunderstood her silence for doubt and reluctance, so continued quickly,

"I mean, no pressure and I would understand if you didn't want to. But I really care for you Eimear, never really felt like this before about anyone and you will be at university in Dublin so we could see each other all the time. I would really love it if I could call you my girlfriend Eimear. But you know… whatever."

Eimear's face had broken into a large grin.

"I would love that more than anything," she had said, much to his pleasure.

As her new boyfriend now lay sleeping peacefully beside her, she replayed this conversation over in her head, smiled to herself, leant over and planted a kiss on Ryan's cheek. She laid her head back down in the crook of his arm and as her eyes started drooping, sleep finally taking her, she let out a contented sigh. She really was very, very happy.

Eimear may have been able to predict that she and Michelle would start to repair their friendship once Eimear admitted she had had sex with Ryan, so excited was she to share the news with her friend. What she did not predict was that having sex would lead to feeling as though she had red hot pokers throwing a party in her bladder every time she urinated.

Why oh why had no one ever told her about cystitis?

As Eimear sat on the toilet for the umpteenth time in an hour, she cursed every woman who had ever had sex before her in the history of the world and had not had the common courtesy to tell her to avoid sex for no other reason than it would make her feel like her urinary tract was slowly decaying.

Although silver lining, she thought as she doubled over on the bathroom floor clutching her sides, nothing fixes a broken friendship like a girl stuck to the toilet like glue.

Michelle could have put Florence Nightingale to shame. She had rushed off to the pharmacy to buy the necessary drugs to ease Eimear's pain and dosed her with pints of water and cranberry juice. When there was no sign of the problem passing, she had driven her to the doctors and had sat with her for two hours in the waiting room, watching invalids who had broken various bones on the mountain, hop or slink in for a consultation with the doctor.

When she had eventually been seen and was prescribed enough drugs to keep her high for a week, they had returned home where, in between Eimear's toilet spells, Michelle had held her hand as they curled up together on the tiny space of the lower bunk and watched chick flick after chick flick in aid of cheering Eimear up.

There had been a few more night-time sessions at Ryan's since that first time but since Eimear felt as though all the sand paper in the world had chosen to erode the internal wall of her bladder, she had only wanted to be around her friend. After discovering that condoms had that effect on girls regularly, Eimear had sworn to never touch men again, a threat which brought a knowing smile to her friend's face.

Since the first time, Eimear and Ryan had become slightly more adventurous. Once she had built her sexual confidence up in the bedroom, Eimear had surprised herself by suggesting that they perhaps explored other venues in which to explore each other, an idea which shocked and excited Ryan.

The couple had moved their sexual encounters elsewhere; locations had included the shower in both Eimear's and Ryan's accommodation (steamy and awkward), the back of Ryan's mini-bus (cold and awkward), a patch of trees on the side of a piste (even colder and slightly exposed; it was not a place either of them rushed to return to) and a jacuzzi outside one of Eimear's company's chalet when it was empty of guests.

Eimear suspected that it was this last place that led to her current crippled state and feared that the frequency at which she and Ryan were having sex was not helping either. The look on Michelle's face when Eimear told her how often they were 'at it' confirmed her suspicions and she swore there and then that she would never have sex again. Or perhaps, just once a week. Or just special occasions. Michelle pressed her lips together tightly and smirked but managed to say nothing.

Since their friendship had been rekindled over a common hatred of cystitis, Eimear and Michelle spent a lot of time discussing sex. Michelle, in all her experience, was far more complimentary about the act whereas Eimear, for whom it was still a bit bizarre, had been known to compare it to seals mating. It wasn't that she hadn't found it pleasurable or 'doing it' in random places exciting. It was just that sex itself was quite... well... undignified. The slappy noises made, the sweat generated, the process of using a condom and even though it disgusted her to admit it, the smell. Sex just was not classy.

In spite of her sceptical views about sex itself, Eimear liked being able to criticise it in this way with her friend. She finally had the knowledge with which to complain and mock; at last, she was no longer on the periphery of these adult, sex-related conversations but could join in with confidence.

And although when she thought about the whole biological side of sex itself she found it a little grotesque, she realised that having it with Ryan was changing her feelings for him. She had always been besotted, as embarrassed as she was to admit it, but now she was feeling something else, something... deeper.

Not only did she feel closer to him and more comfortable around him, she found herself day-dreaming about parts of her life that were way in the future but now they featured him by her side. When she realised what she was doing she would quickly shake herself out of it and swear on all that was sacred in the world that she would not have those thoughts again. But secretly, she found herself hoping that he would meet her family; she would picture him sitting around the table getting interrogated and mocked by her brothers, a standard initiating procedure anyone new went through.

She imagined introducing him to her friends and, when she moved up to study in Dublin, going out for nice meals with him in O'Connell Street. Sleeping with Ryan and hearing him make assertions about his feelings for her was giving her hope that maybe their relationship would extend past the ski season.

One relationship that was not rectified, however, was that between her and her bosses. Every time she saw them, she felt an urge to flee, and she realised that they probably felt the same, wondering why they were still employing her. Maybe she just wasn't cut out to be a chalet girl.

In fact, Eimear was surprised to find that she really was starting to look forward to returning home and had already started to count down the days until she was back in the bosom of her much-missed family.

CHAPTER 22

The latest guests were... interesting. To call the group 'yuppie airheads' would be doing both yuppies and airheads around the world an injustice.

Eimear and Michelle could not believe that evolution had not done its bit in weeding out this particular breed of stupid from the human race. The morons just did not seem to understand that life differed outside of a city and that, when in a foreign country, the culture, language, food and even life itself, would vary.

Eimear and Michelle had quickly learnt that meal times and eating habits were quite revealing of people's odd behaviour and personalities, and their odd food requests even more so. On the first day, one of their new guests complained that the girls had not provided him with cornflakes at breakfast. After showing him the large bowl of cornflakes that was placed quite obviously on the breakfast table so that he would be able to help himself, he responded 'they are not proper cornflakes, they are French cornflakes.'

Eimear, the unfortunate recipient of this odd request, had just stared at him.

Really? she thought, French cornflakes? In France? How odd. And there was she thinking that Kellogg's imported crate loads of cornflakes personally to her chalet as obviously nowhere else in the world was capable of making that particular cereal. Thank God he was able to clear up the confusion regarding the ethnicity of the food. That had been giving her sleepless nights.

All she could do was bite her tongue, nod sympathetically and point out that yes, they were French, but cornflakes will pretty much tasted the same no matter which passport they owned. Poor sod, she had thought to herself as she watched him gingerly pour milk onto his non-Kellogg's cornflakes, to be plagued with so many serious worries.

At the group's first meal, one of their party requested that

they had ketchup with their starter. Bemused as to how someone could eat ketchup with soup, Michelle had returned to the
kitchen, scooped ketchup into a ceramic bowl and returned to
the dining table to place the bowl beside the guest. Whilst the
two girls stood over the cooker preparing the main course,
they snuck the odd look over their shoulder to see how this
ingredient added to the flavour of carrot and coriander soup.
In horror, they watched as the guest spread a thick layer of
ketchup over the freshly chopped baguette and dunked it into
the soup. They could barely control their gag reflexes. But it
did not stop there; the bowl of ketchup had to be topped up for
every course and this atrocity occurred every evening for the
remainder of the group's stay. Prawn salad for starter, ketchup
on the side. Lamb for main, ketchup on the side. Chocolate
brownies for dessert, better leave the ketchup on the side, just
in case. Steaks, chicken, duck, goat's cheese tarts, boiled potatoes, roasted potatoes, lentils and couscous.

All had the complimentary ceramic, decorative ketchup
bowl on the side. There really was no questioning taste.

The girls had started a 'Dumbass of the Day' award between
themselves and whichever guest's antics bemused them the
most, they were granted this prestigious award. That day's
winner had really impressed the girls this time and had even
managed to surpass the stupidity of any of the other skiing
party that week. At four o'clock that afternoon, before the time
the guests had been told they could contact the girls to request
a lift, Eimear had received a call on her mobile. Sighing as she
saw the number was not a French one, therefore could only
mean one thing, Eimear had chucked her phone at Michelle
and gestured to her to answer it. After letting the guest speak
for a moment, Michelle had stifled her giggles and put the
phone on loud speaker so Eimear could listen in too.

"... it is just that I hadn't quite anticipated how long the run
was," the guest wittered on, "so if you could be so kind as to
call me a taxi, I will just sit here on the side of the run and wait
for it to come and get me."

Eimear released one of her less than attractive snorts.

Gesturing frantically at Eimear to shut up, Michelle managed to compose herself enough to explain,

"I am afraid we don't have taxis for the ski slopes. You are just going to have to come down by yourself."

"What about one of those snow mobile things?" the guest enquired.

"They are for private hire for special tours or are booked in advance."

"Yes, but I have seen loads of those scooters take people down the mountains in those cool orange bed things."

"Um..." hesitated Michelle, "they are stretchers. Usually designed for those who have broken something and can't ski down. Or who have died." She tried to add helpfully.

"So you won't call me one?" the guest asked again, petulance lacing her voice.

"I am really sorry but I cannot call you a ski taxi as they don't actually exist. From the sounds of it though, you aren't too far from the bottom of the run. Have a break and then go again. You will be home before you know it."

After hanging up the phone the girls had dissolved into fits of giggles. At dinner that night they had to suppress even more bursts of laughter as they listened to the guests complain that there were no such things as ski taxis driving around the slopes for tired skiers to summon.

While the taxi request was completely idiotic, Eimear wasn't sure if her intolerance was because her guests were really just stupid or whether she was just tired. As they approached the end of March and only had a few weeks left, everything just felt like more of an effort now. She realised she no longer had the enthusiasm or the energy which she had at the start of the season.

Getting up at half 6 or 7 every morning now felt like a form of torture; meeting new guests and showing interest in their stories no longer came easily to the girls. Even skiing felt like less fun as the weather started to become spring-like and the snow started to become more sluggish. Eimear found she was making more and more excuses to not go up the mountain.

After doing her morning chores, which now took longer than ever before as she could not muster any enthusiasm, she found that she just could not be bothered to ski and either went back to bed to catch up on much needed sleep or wandered through the streets with her friends checking out the end of season sales and finding yet another coffee shop to drink in.

It wasn't that she no longer loved L'Homme; she still found beauty in the mountains and the sunlight when it fell on the snow. On the rare occasions she forced herself to ski, she still felt a huge thrill as she whizzed down the mountain at a speed and ability she had not thought possible at the beginning of the season.

It was just that, and she was not alone in this as, having spoken to her friends about it she discovered they too felt it, she was absolutely exhausted. Months of partying, skiing hard and working harder had finally taken its toll.

One night, as she lay beside Ryan after having sex (she had decided that her return to full health should be classed as a special occasion) she had tried to discuss her feelings with him.

"I love L'Homme," she mused, "but I can feel myself getting more and more impatient with my life here. I find myself counting down the days until the end of the season and I just can't wait to go home, to have a bit of normality. I see the guests packing up at the end of the week and I find myself envious of their imminent return to their everyday lives. I mean, it just isn't real life here, is it?"

She looked over at Ryan to see his response and was shocked to see that he looked as though she had punched him in the face.

"Don't be so ridiculous Eimear," he snapped. "This place is paradise, what more could you want here? Go to sleep, I have to be up early in the morning."

He leant over her, pressed the lamp switch with such vigour he knocked it off the side of his bed stand and turned his back on her, suggesting the conversation was over.

Eimear stared at his back for a few moments in silent shock

before trying to turn her back on him without falling out of his tiny bed. As she was left alone in the dark with her thoughts, she could not supress the feeling that something just wasn't quite right, that change was imminent and it wasn't necessarily going to be the results she wanted.

CHAPTER 23

When Ryan's alarm went off that morning, Eimear hoped for some sort of affectionate gesture from him to show that he was sorry for snapping at her. But none came.

I'll be damned if I'm making the first move to reconcile the situation when he is being the irrational one, the arsehole, she stubbornly told herself.

With the mood strained, they both dressed for work without saying a word or even looking at each other. By the time she was ready to leave, the tension was palpable. She made her way to the bedroom door and hesitated for a moment; she had never left without giving him a goodbye kiss. But glancing towards him, she saw that his back was turned from her, shoulders hunched as though protecting himself from any sort of contact.

Irritation flooded her and she left the room without as much as a nod in his direction.

She didn't understand it; was he pissed off just because she had dared criticise the precious life style of a seasonaire? If so, he needed to get a bloody grip.

But for all of her stubbornness and determination to make him see the error of his ways, she couldn't help feeling more and more forlorn as the day went on and she didn't hear from him.

For once, Eimear was relieved that it was 'change over' day, the day when the old set of guests left the chalet and the new ones arrived. Depending on when the guests left and how soon the next ones arrived, the day could often be very hectic as you had to 'change over' the chalet in a matter of hours ahead of the group's arrival. On this occasion, girls only had two hours to strip the beds, completely clean the chalet, remake the rooms and get the dinner started before the Robinsons, a family of four, arrived. She threw herself into the cleaning and, except for the odd check of her phone, didn't have time to dwell on the bizarre conversation from the night before too much.

When the Robinsons arrived, Eimear and Michelle were glad to see that they looked relatively normal. Their little boys, aged four and two, seemed really cute and didn't look as though they would cause any hassle.

The sight of children always brought joy to the chalet hosts. The company's cooking rules dictated that the staff had to cook 'posh meals' for their guests, not dishes that could be found on the mountain. Dishes such as carbonara, spaghetti bolognaise or chips and chicken nuggets were therefore a definite no-no… unless children were in the chalet and then it was acceptable to cook such meals as their taste buds often preferred simple meals. After months of eating 'semi-gourmet' meals (by Eimear's and Michelle's standards, so not that gourmet at all) with their guests, they craved simple meals such as those served on the mountain.

For the Robinsons' children, they cooked enough spaghetti bolognaise to feed an army. After serving it to them, they returned to the kitchen and ravaged the pot like lions destroying a carcass. Once they had had their fill, they busied themselves with finalising the preparation for the adults' meal. The parents put their children to bed and took their places at the dining room table where they looked at the newly set four places with some confusion.

Not thinking much of it, she and Michelle carried the starters over to the table and then took their seats beside the Robinsons. Having just demolished a whole pan of spaghetti bolognaise, they weren't that hungry so only gave themselves half of the goat cheese tartlet each.

Michelle poured the wine into all of the glasses and, as was custom, raised her glass in a toast.

"Here's to a fanta…"

Her voice died mid-sentence. The Robinsons' had not raised their glasses; they both looked really uncomfortable and were avoiding eye contact with the girls by staring down into their tarts.

"Everything ok?" Michelle asked

"Um…" Mr Robinson started after a pregnant pause. "We don't mean this rudely but… what are you doing sitting at the table?"

Michelle and Eimear looked at each other. Well, this was awkward.

Eimear explained that it was company policy for staff to eat with their guests.

"Right..." said Mr Robinson. "But can you not?"

Neither Michelle nor Eimear quite knew how to respond. Choosing to say nothing, they stood, picked up their plates and returned to the kitchen. There they remained for the rest of the meal, putting the plates down in front of their guests before returning to the kitchen to pick at the various courses.

"Rude weirdos!" Michelle mouthed to Eimear over the Eton mess dessert.

When they left the chalet that night, Eimear noticed she had a text from Ryan asking her to call him. She did so after what she thought was a suitable waiting time to make him sweat a bit.

When he answered the phone, the tension from the night before and that morning was not evident in his voice. He started chatting away like normal and didn't hint to the fight; it was as though it had never happened. Confused and needing to talk about it properly, Eimear eventually enquired as to why she hadn't heard from him all day. His response was pretty nonchalant, saying he had been busy and that she hadn't been in touch with him either. When she then tried to bring up the argument, he snapped at her, telling her it was just a silly fight and that she needed to move on.

The next few days were no different but it was clear to everyone they were not getting on as well as normal. The Robinsons had called the Devil-Bosses to request that the girls did not eat with them for the rest of the week. Apparently, they did not see each other much at home due to their jobs so this was an opportunity to rekindle their fire. The girls knew what that meant; they would be changing those sheets regularly throughout the week. As a result of the arrangement, the girls were delighted to hear that they now had their evenings free. All they had to do was prepare the food for the family in the morning and then the Robinsons would reheat it when they wanted it that night.

Without having to return to work in the evening, Eimear and

Ryan ended up having more time together. Pre-argument, this would have filled Eimear with joy. However, all they seemed to do was irritate each other. Any time she mentioned something about looking forward to going home or that she felt like she was living in a bubble, he got very defensive and they would end up snapping at each other. In return, any time Eimear heard him talking about his life in L'Homme and how sad he would be when he left, all which was said with a pathetically wistful gaze on his face, she got annoyed and would say anything in an attempt to burst his paradisiacal bubble. It was not a characteristic she liked about herself and would end up annoyed with him for bringing it out in her. Either way, Eimear concluded, their arguments were definitely all his fault.

On the day before their day off, Eimear and Michelle decided to have a girly day together up the mountain once they had sorted the Robinsons' meal out. Eimear was somewhat surprised to find that she was pleased to not be with Ryan, the implications of which, she realised, did not bode well for them.

On their way down the mountain that afternoon, she received a phone call from Ryan who had been drinking since noon as none of his guests required his services. Hearing how drunk he was already by 5 o'clock, she got irritated with him again. Her feeling of exasperation was perpetuated when he got arsey with her for not wanting to join him in 'getting lashed'.

"Look Ryan, we're all going out tonight ok? So I will see you in Binky's, assuming you make it out. You're pretty half cut by the sounds of things so drink some water."

"Oh, whatever Eimear. I'll see you around, maybe."

And with that, he hung up the phone. Rolling her eyes, she told Michelle about the conversation.

"I'm sure he'll twist that into some sort of criticism of his lifestyle here. I just don't want to start drinking too early! I'm sure I am getting liver failure from all this drinking you know, I think it was hurting me the other day. It's just quite nice to take it easy for once."

"I don't blame you," Michelle comforted her friend. "I don't think I am going to have a mad one tonight either. Come on, let's go and put face masks on for tonight. We are going to look beeeeaaaauuuutiful."

She put her arm around her friend and took her inside The Palace. She didn't want to tell Eimear, but she didn't think their arguments were a good sign of things to come. But for now, all she could do was pamper Eimear to cheer her up and she was determined to do a damn good job of it.

CHAPTER 24

The sound of a phone ringing roused Eimear from her deep slumber. Without raising her head or opening her eyes she started feeling around her bed looking for the errant phone. She had a vague recollection of scrolling through all the messages Ryan had ever sent her before falling asleep, so she knew it had to be nearby.

The ringing stopped before she located it so she let her arm drop over her eyes and started to drift off to sleep once more. Just as she could feel all of her limbs start to relax as she began drifting off, the ringing started again. This time, feeling highly disgruntled that her precious lie-in was being disturbed, she leant up on her elbows and glanced around the room through squinted eyes, ears straining. The ringing appeared to be coming from in-between the wall and the side of the bed. Realising she must have knocked it in her sleep, she swung down from her bed onto Michelle's, wiggled her arm into the tiny gap and started rooting around.

Many stray socks, hair bobbles, a pair of dirty knickers and an empty condom wrapper later, Eimear found her phone which lay silent once again. Eimear chucked the blue tin-foiled wrapper onto the floor; Michelle had obviously been taking advantage of the nights Eimear had been staying over at Ryan's. She would be having a stern word with her friend about cleaning up properly after herself. She dreaded to think what else might be down there.

Through blurry eyes she saw that the incessant caller had been her mother. I'll call her back later, Eimear thought as she snuggled down into Michelle's bed, too lazy to climb back into her own in spite of a slight concern that she was sleeping on skanky sheets. God knows what or whose juices she was sleeping on.

The phone started ringing for a third time.

"For the love of God!" Eimear exclaimed before grumpily answering,

"Lo?"

"Well isn't it lovely to hear the enthusiasm and joy in my only daughter's voice when she speaks to her loving mother who misses her with all her heart and soul."

Eimear sighed and rolled her eyes. Her mum was in one of those moods.

"Hi mum. I'm sleeping. What do you want?"

"You have post."

If looks could kill. Eimear removed her phone from her ear and mouthed an expletive at it whilst glaring at the caller I.D. before returning to the phone call. She had never been a good morning person.

"You woke me up to tell me I had post?"

"It's not any old post you ungrateful rogue. It's from University College Dublin. I assumed you would want to know what it said. But I'll just go shall I, since I am interrupting your much needed beauty sleep.

Eimear's attention was caught, so much so that she didn't even notice the insult her mother had doled out to her.

That was the first correspondence she had had from her future university since she had had her place confirmed the previous summer.

"Can you open it please? What does it say?"

"Hmmmm I thought as much," her mum sounded smug.

Eimear could hear an envelope being torn open down the other end of the phone and found she was suddenly quite nervous. She clutched her knotted stomach to try and ease the churning. She hadn't given that stage of her life much thought while she had been away playing in the mountains.

Her mother's phone call had brought her crashing back to reality.

"It's just a 'keeping in touch' letter," her mum said after a short silence. "They are letting you know when they will be in touch about accommodation and your course texts. Ooh, they have even included some leaflets of the campus and different accommodation options. Very nice."

Eimear could hear her mother flicking through the various bits of paperwork. "Do I have to do anything with it mum?" She asked, wishing she could see it for herself. The nerves had been replaced with excitement and she wanted to know more.

"Nope, not for now. I'll keep them for you and we'll look through it all when you get home."

Eimear felt an overwhelming urge to be there now, sitting at the kitchen table with her mum, papers spread out over an already cluttered kitchen table, tea in hand. Not for the first time she once again wished that the season would hurry up and end.

"Come here to me, what's this I hear about a boyfriend?"

Eimear was stunned.

Thousands of miles away and still her mother was able to keep tabs on her. She really was omnipresent. Eimear stupidly found herself glancing around the room, as though she expected her mum to pop her head around the door and announce that she had been there the whole time. She wouldn't put it past her mum actually.

"How did you...?" Eimear spluttered, her face turning a flourescent shade of red.

"Facebook." Her mum said, very matter of fact. "If you don't want me to know stuff then you shouldn't put it online. Your brothers wanted some money to go out so we did a deal. Payment for gossip. I think this may be the best deal we have done yet."

Eimear mentally cursed her brothers. She would find a way to stitch them right up when she got home.

"Why can't they get normal jobs like other people?" she wailed.

"Apparently gossip is far more lucrative for them. I admit I am not imparting the best values in them by doing this but I get great news out of it.

"Right, anyway. Don't digress. I take by your lack of denial that this is true?"

Eimear hesitated; she was a crap liar at the best of times but when it came to her mum, she found it even harder to do. The woman had a creepy ability see through any untruth.

But she need not have worried; the hesitation had been all the confirmation her mother had needed.

"Well I never," her mum guffawed. "What will your father say?"

"Oh please don't wind me up Mama, it's not that big a deal!"

"Are you sleeping with him?"

Eimear's face rapidly drained of the colour her cheeks had so quickly filled with only moments before. This constant fluctuation of blood flow into and out of her face could not be good for her. She felt as though she had been punched in the stomach and was slightly breathless as she tried to work out her response,

What could she say? The woman had skills similar to that of an SAS interrogator so she could, and oh she would, get the truth out of her daughter eventually.

But she had to try and lie, Eimear told herself with absolute certainty. This was one thing she could not and should not be honest about, not yet anyway. Not until she was married and had had at least two children, all of whom she would initially claim were the gifts of storks.

"Of course not mum!"

"So yes then."

"What? How have you worked that one out?"

"I can hear it in your voice."

"You cannot!"

"Yes, I can. Anyway!" She raised her voice over her daughter's high-pitched protestations. "All you youngsters are at it these days. I've learnt that from your brothers too."

Eimear was really going to have to end these Facebook payoffs when she got home.

"I'll send you some condoms in the post, just in case. I think Donnacha has some in his drawer."

"Mum, there really is no need and by the way, that offer is wrong on so many levels."

"Your father is calling on the other line pet, I have got to go." Her mother clearly was not listening to a word she was saying. "He has probably mislaid something again and will expect me to use my magical powers of telepathy to work out where he left it. That man will be the death of me if you lot don't end me first. I'll send you that little parcel and I want it on record that, if you

156

are, and I think we both know the truth, I disapprove. You can't give it away again you know, once you have done it then that's it. That person is going to have a connection with you for life. And FYI, I do not want any teenage pregnancies in my house. Got to go, love you, au revoir!"

And she was gone. Eimear held her phone in the palm of her hand in a daze. That was the most bizarre conversation she had ever had in her life. She wasn't quite sure what had just happened. Was her mother actually going to send her condoms? Worse, condoms which belonged to her big brother?

Michelle walked through their bedroom door and found Eimear staring at her phone in bewilderment. Her friend had picked up one of her regular 'friends' the night before at Binky's and had gone back to his place. She looked surprised to see her.

"Hello, I wasn't expecting to find you here, I thought you were staying at Ryan's," she said as she crawled into the bottom bunk and curled her cold legs around Eimear's warm ones.

"I was but we ended up having a massive row so I came home. I couldn't be arsed with him."

By the time Eimear had seen him in Binky's that night, Ryan could barely stand. Disgusted by the state he was in and in an attempt to give her liver a rest, she had got them both a drink of water and tried to encourage him to have some. As predicted, Ryan took Eimear's admission of disgust and lack of drink as an implicit criticism of the ski season lifestyle. The tension and bickering from the last few days, fuelled and far more vicious than normal thanks to the drink, erupted in the street outside of Binky's.

"I just left him in the street in the end and walked home," Eimear finished off after telling Michelle the whole thing. "I just could not be bothered with it, it is making me feel exhausted."

"Have you heard from him today?" Michelle asked.

"Are you joking? He was so drunk he won't surface for hours. I hope his head really hurts," she added, somewhat vindictively and bitterly.

"Anyway, I have his phone. He kept dropping it so I put it in my bag for him before we fell out. I completely forgot I had it until I got home. He'll probably wake up today and think he has lost it. The tool.

"Anyway, how was your night?"

"Fine, the usual, you know. Doing the walk of shame wasn't fun this morning though, especially not in this bloody centurion outfit." Michelle gestured to the sheet she had wrapped herself in the night before for Binky's fancy dress party. "I was freezing walking home and I bumped into Lucy and Ian on the way back. You should have seen the way they looked at me. They just smirked and then crossed over the road to avoid talking to me. Fine by me, obviously."

The two girls rolled their eyes and snuggled down a little bit further under the quilt.

"Why do you think Ryan is being so tetchy?" Michelle asked after a few moments.

"Dunno," Eimear responded after a bit of thought. "Maybe it is because he is leaving at the end of this season. You know his parents are putting pressure on him to move back?"

Michelle nodded.

"Well I think it is starting to dawn on him and I think it scares him. He has done this for so long that going back to get a 'real' job is going to be a bit of a shock to the system."

"Emsie… do you think he will go back? I know he will have you which will help… but has he started putting plans into place? Like looking for a job? Or even booking a flight?"

"No… but he definitely will… I mean…. Well he has promised."

But both girls could hear that lack of certainty in Eimear's voice. She was needing to convince herself as much if not more than her friend.

For the first time since she had got together with Ryan, doubt that their relationship could be anything but perfect had started to creep into her mind.

CHAPTER 25

The girls got into their onesies, went to the communal kitchen and cooked a fry-up fit for kings. All of the ingredients were acquired courtesy of Lucy's and Ian's budget, little to their knowledge, a fact that gave the team great satisfaction. They had to get their kicks and revenge where they could.

Once they'd had their fill they returned to Michelle's bunk, curled up in their respective quilts, stuck a chick flick on the laptop and proceeded to chat all the way through it.

Eimear told Michelle about the conversation she had with her mother and her friend erupted in laughter.

"Your mum is brilliant and an actual genius. She knows full well how awkward that would have made you! It is the perfect contraception as you could never use those condoms without thinking of her and your brother. In fact, next time you try and get jiggy with it I bet they will pop into your head and it will make you feel very uncomfortable. I think you should thank Donnacha by the way.

"He has obviously desensitised your mum to that sort of behaviour!" she added quickly in response to Eimear's perplexed and somewhat hostile look.

"By the sounds of all the practice he is getting I may need to hang out a bit more at your house when we get back. I bet he is becoming a right fox in the sack..." she added teasingly before taking cover underneath the quilt, pre-empting Eimear's pillow which would inevitably be chucked at her.

After the scuffling and wind-ups about Eimear's brothers died down, and Eimear's pillow had been returned to its owner, conversation turned to their plans after the season which was a mere four weeks away.

"I am thinking of doing something in America, maybe a tour or Camp America," Michelle mused. "I'm not sure yet, just want to do one more trip before uni starts. You?"

"Ryan and I have talked about going on holiday or something. Then getting a job to save some money for the start of term I guess. I am quite jealous of your idea though Mitch," she said forlornly. "Sounds pretty cool."

"Well why don't you come with me Emsie? We could plan it together?"

A knock at the door interrupted their conversation.

"Come in!" Michelle bellowed, causing Eimear to flinch slightly.

"Jesus Christ woman, you are so loud!" she said, booting her friend in the back in mock anger.

A ginormous bunch of flowers entered the room with only the carrier's legs visible beneath them. Eimear recognised those scuffed shoes and, her heart beat increasing ever so slightly, she found it hard to stop the smile which had started to form at the corner of her lips.

She hadn't wanted to admit it to Michelle but the lack of contact from her boyfriend had started to alarm her and she had been checking Facebook subtly on her phone, assuming that he would try to contact her via it given his phoneless situation.

Seeing the bouquet walk through the door eased the anxious knot which had been developing in her stomach throughout the morning and she could feel relief seeping through her body.

Michelle winked at her from the end of the bed. "Alright Ryan? How's the head? Heard it was a mad one last night." She received another boot in the back.

"Anyhow," she carried on, "I was just about to make a cuppa. Anyone want one?" And with that, she hopped out of bed, squeezed past the bunch of flowers and was gone before hearing anyone's answer.

The legs beneath the flowers started to shuffle from side to side. A pair of eyes peaked over the top and looked around the room at everything but Eimear.

Eimear readjusted her position in the bed so she was sitting more comfortably. She had a feeling this was going to take a while and she would be damned if she was going to break the silence first.

After a lot more foot shuffling and eye glancing, Ryan cleared his throat. "May I?"

The bouquet of flowers was thrust towards Michelle's recently vacated spot.

"Be my guest," Eimear replied, moving her legs as she did to allow him to perch on the bed.

Silence resumed. Eimear started to twiddle her thumbs. This was getting boring. She found herself humming 'It's a small world after all' in her head. It certainly was not making the situation any better.

Eventually, Ryan turned so he was facing her and, head slumped, he uttered, "I am so, so sorry. I hear I was a bit of a knob last night."

"A bit." Eimear said. She was annoyed with herself for starting to get upset as the episodes from last night came rushing back to her. She had sworn she wouldn't allow them to affect her, but appear indifferent to it all. She hadn't told Michelle everything, pride hadn't let her, but Ryan had said some pretty horrible things to her last night, including that he didn't see the point in them anymore.

"I really am so sorry Eimear. I was so drunk and I don't really remember what happened. If it is any consolation, I have the hangover of my life and feel as though I am dying. I also think I punched the wall as my hand is in agony."

He lifted it up so she could inspect it. His knuckles were a weird purple colour and she could see cuts amongst the swelling.

Good, she thought, that will teach him to drink so much and behave like a moron.

He had scared her a little as she had never seen that side of him before. He had always been so collected and dignified, even when drunk. At most, he was funny, kind and soppy when having a few, not angry like last night. She had realised there was still so much to learn about the Adonis before her, whom she had thought she knew so well.

"Gin," he said, as though reading her mind. "I have never been good on it and apparently, using it as my drink of choice for the extended drinking binge brought out my arsehole side. I really am so, so sorry."

"You said you couldn't be bothered with me anymore," she

said, biting her quivering lip in an attempt to stop herself from showing any emotion. Much to her annoyance, she could do nothing about the tears welling up in her eyes.

A look of absolute horror crossed Ryan's face and to her shock, his eyes started filling up too.

"Oh my God Eimear, I didn't, did I? I am really sorry, I can't believe I even said that. You know I didn't mean it though don't you?" he said, dropping the flowers on her bed and grabbing her hands. "Eimear please, look at me, you must know I didn't mean that!"

He lifted her chin and looked into her tear-filled eyes. Pulling her into a bear hug he shook his head and whispered, "I have never felt about anyone how I how feel about you. I cannot believe I said that, I am so angry with myself."

Eimear nodded to show that she was listening but didn't trust herself to speak.

"Look, let me take you to dinner tonight to make it up to you, ok? Then we can talk it all through properly. Would you like that?"

Eimear nodded. This was possibly the longest she had ever been silent.

"Ok well I'll go and ring around some places to see where is free and will text you so you know when to be ready ok? I'll come and pick you up and then take you into town."

"You'll be needing this then." She rooted around in her handbag, found his dead phone and chucked it at him.

He looked confused. "How do you have this? I didn't even notice it was gone!"

"You were having some difficulty with your hands last night," she said with a slight smile. "I thought it was safer if I looked after it for you. Of course, that was before I decided I hated you a little bit."

Ryan matched her smile. "I would have hated me too by the sounds of things. Thanks for looking after my phone. I think I had better sleep for a bit too if I am going to be able to wine and dine my girl to the best of my ability."

A knock at the door signalled that Michelle wanted to come

back in so Ryan stood but not before giving her a lingering kiss on her lips.

"Does tonight sound ok to you then?"

"It's a plan," Eimear nodded.

"Right, well I'll be in touch then." And with that, he bent down, gave her another soft kiss and left the room.

CHAPTER 26

Ryan booked them a table in the popular restaurant, Mangeons. It was one that they had frequented, as had many a seasonaire and holiday-dweller alike. It was a picturesque restaurant with old farming pictures and antique farming equipment on the walls, reminding all that L'Homme always had been and still was an authentic farming town. Scattered between the frames and wooden scythes were candles in beautiful brass holders built into the wall to give a genuine atmospheric feel to the restaurant. The mood lighting and reasonably priced menu meant the restaurant was always busy but somehow, Ryan had succeeded in using his prestige to get them, not only a table, but one in a particularly romantic spot.

He was really making an effort tonight, Eimear noticed. He had turned up at The Palace at seven o'clock on the dot, dressed in his best outfit. She hadn't been able to help but take a lingering look at his bulging biceps in his figure-hugging top, nor the pert buttocks in his jeans. He had asked one of his colleagues, Bruce, to give him a lift to Eimear's and on arrival, had opened the door for her into the van. Similarly, when Bruce pulled up outside Mangeons, Ryan had hopped out before the van had come to a complete stand-still to make sure he had reached her door in enough time to continue his chivalrous act.

Once inside, they had been ushered to the secluded table in Ryan's chosen atmospheric spot and left to study their menus.

"Wine?" Ryan asked after a while.

"Yeah that would be nice, as long as you think you can stomach it," Eimear said, running her eyes over the wine list, not understanding any of the descriptions.

'Blended from the juiciest sun-drenched grapes this rich, full-bodied red is loaded with dark berry aromas and has a subtle hint of spice' she read before hesitating. What the... full-bodied? What was that supposed to taste like? And what would the alternative be? 'Dark berry aromas'? Like what, blackberries?

Wine really was a drink for the more superior taste buds she decided, and started looking at price as an indicator instead.

"I think the Shiraz sounds nice, what do you think?" Ryan asked looking up from his menu.

Eimear's eyes drifted to the price. 25€? She gulped slightly; the price differed somewhat from her usual 5€ Jagerbombs. He must have seen the look on her face because he leant over the table and grasped her hand.

"Tonight is on me, ok? I want to make it up to you after my terrible behaviour last night."

Eimear hesitated; she knew it was stupid but she didn't feel comfortable with how the evening was panning out. The fine wine, the intimate table, the chivalrous acts and fancy clothing, they all made her feel worse. The extent he was going to indicated a severe admission of guilt; had he just finished at the flowers, or even suggested a chat over a drink that evening, she would have been able to belittle the argument, making it feel insignificant. Splashing out so much made her face reality; they were not in a good place and it was pretty obvious that cracks were starting to appear in the very relationship she thought was perfect.

A feeling of melancholy descended upon her and she looked into her lap at her hands.

"Hey," Ryan said softly, "You ok?"

Was she? Was she just deceiving herself by trying to convincing herself that this was something that could work outside their L'Homme bubble? She felt stupid and ridiculously sad. The things he had said to her last night must have come from some subconscious thought and maybe, she should just accept this for what it was and not try to make more of it. Perhaps, after all, they were just a ski season romance. A great one admittedly, but that was all. But she wanted it to be more; she knew she would be distraught if she had to leave at the end of the season knowing that it was the end of them.

"Eimear."

She looked up at the sound of Ryan's voice and he was alarmed to see that her big, beautiful blue eyes had tears rolling from them and down her gorgeous, freckled cheeks.

"Hey," he said, wiping the tears away. "I was an idiot last night. Is that what you are upset about?"

"Ryan, maybe we need to accept that you are meant to stay here and that we are just a ski season relationship which has a 'best before' date."

"Stop that right now," he said firmly. "I know that there is no excusing what I did or what I said but I was just a drunken, ginned-up fool. I know I said I couldn't be bothered with us but surely doing all of this for you shows that I really am bothered by you, by us? I admit I am nervous about the end of the season and leaving this all for good. But my parents are right, I have to leave Neverland and grow up at some point. It is them I should be taking it out on as they are the ones forcing me into adulthood, not you." He gave her a wry smile.

Initially comforted by his words, Eimear thought for a moment. Something he said put a seed of doubt in her mind. Why should he be taking his mood out on anyone? Saying that suggested he was being made to leave against his will and, if he had a choice, he would not be leaving at all. Eimear had always known that his parents were putting him under pressure but, perhaps naively, she was under the impression he didn't mind coming back because they got to stay together.

She said as much to him.

"But… you know I would love to stay. You know this is my idea of heaven. But my parents are putting the pressure on so I've got to go back, for a while at least, to appease them. They have said that they won't help me stay out here anymore. You know, send me money when I need it. So I have to go back, for a while at least, until I have earned enough money to come back out here for good. The only silver lining is that I don't lose you at the end of the season. You know that would break my heart."

Eimear wasn't sure what to think about this. She no longer doubted or feared how he felt about her but something still wasn't feeling right. Now, however, was not the time to think about it, she decided.

She gave him a small smile and squeezed his hand back. "Ok then, let's order shall we?" she said a little too brightly.

Ryan ordered the wine and when it was delivered to the table, he poured a glass for them both.

"To us!" he toasted with revived confidence.

Eimear smiled, said nothing, tapped his glass and took a sip. She really did know nothing about wine.

Later on that night, after they had had make-up sex, very good sex too she acknowledged, she lay in the crook of his arm. As he slept soundly besides her, she was able to think properly over their conversation.

It was going to be ok, she concluded. So he wasn't thrilled about going back and thought that one day, he would return to the resort. But he was definitely returning to Ireland for now and who knows, maybe he would change his mind once he spent some time at home. More importantly, he was mad about her and this was something she felt confident about. The words he had spoken that evening, the care he had shown her, his profuse apologies for their argument, it all proved to her that he did care, and cared a lot.

As she closed her eyes and snuggled in more closely to his warm body and she tried to get some sleep, an alarming and doubt-ridden thought crept into her mind.

Yes, he did care about her, but was it ever going to be enough to make this work outside of the paradisiacal bubble that was L'Homme?

CHAPTER 27

As much as she tried, it took Eimear a while to shift the feeling of doubt that had descended upon her after she and Ryan had had the row. She tried to tell herself that she was being a pessimist and that everything was going to be ok. But something told her it wasn't.

But after a full two weeks of Ryan continually reassuring her, unprovoked, that he cared about her and not once complaining about having to go home, she started to feel confident in them once again. They didn't talk about their fight again, or even what they were going to do once they got back to Ireland. It felt as though it was too much to discuss yet; they just needed to get back on track, to just enjoy being 'them' again. Anyway, there would be plenty of time to discuss those plans once they did return to Ireland. As it was, the end of the season was quickly encroaching and Eimear decided she didn't want to waste what little time they had in this environment, fretting over a silly argument.

Eimear and Michelle felt a mixture of emotions as they cooked their final meal for their last set of guests in the chalet. Elation that they would not have to cook again and that they would be seeing their friends and family soon, a sense of achievement at surviving the season and through it all, a great sense of sadness that soon, it would all be over.

As guests went, this group were quite low maintenance. Eimear and Michelle did not have to do or say much for the group to have a good time. They had not complained once, even when the girls forgot to put chicken in the chicken risotto. For this, both Eimear and Michelle were immensely relieved. They did not think they had the tolerance or the energy for a high maintenance group, not at this stage of the season.

As the girls turned the oven off and wiped down the kitchen for the last post-dinner clean-up of the season, they took a moment to glance around. So much of their season had been based around this room; the menu planning sessions, the squabbles over who had moved their shopping account card from its usual place or had left a dirty pot in the sink, panic because they had not done their weekly budget check and they did not think they had time to do it in the five minutes before Lucy came over for their usual meeting from hell. The numerous breakfasts, afternoon cakes and dinners, all of various degrees of success, which they had cooked for their guests who had ranged from the ridiculously fun to the unimaginably difficult. The room had been the hub of activity for the season and it was odd to think they would not be cooking another meal for a set of guests again.

Eimear and Michelle left the kitchen and went into the den to say goodbye to their guests; they did not require breakfast as they had an inhumanely early transfer booked to the airport so the girls would not be seeing them again. Joe, the eldest member of the group, thrust 30€ into Michelle's hand as they stood beside the door to leave.

"We've had a great week girls, thank you for looking after us so well. We'll be sure to pass our compliments onto your managers. Buy yourself a drink or two on us."

Eimear and Michelle were shocked and touched; they had not had many tips throughout the season, something they hoped was not reflective of their hosting skills. Perhaps just the recession, they told themselves. As for passing good feedback onto the Devil's wing man and wing woman, they were both sure it would give their managers heart attacks.

"Here's hoping anyway," Michelle said to Eimear with an awkward giggle.

The girls exchanged a bemused look before quickly changing the subject. Discussing guests' thoughts and feedback still made the two of them feel slightly uneasy since the mishap with Lucy, even though they had made up.

As they piled into the mini-bus to head back to The Palace, with Mark behind the wheel, conversation turned to the prospect of hitting the town to celebrate the last night of guests.

"Binky's?" a voice suggested.

Where else?

Eimear woke up the next morning curled up in the corner of

Ryan's bed thanks to his sprawled out, heavily sleeping body. She smiled to herself and watched him sleep. It had been a fun night with everyone doing stupid dances on the dance floor and ending up in the club once Binky's closed. She felt sorry for those in her team who had to get up this morning and make breakfast for the last time of the season; they would not be feeling good.

Her phone pinged so she leant over Ryan's exposed leg and grabbed it from the floor.

Fancy hitting the slopes?

Last day of the resort being open, you had better!

All of the guests have now gone, we don't need to start our deep cleaning yet...

Leave your hunk of a man in bed and get your butt back home now.

Leaving soon.

Emma x

I'm in, Eimear texted back before digging Ryan in the side, who grunted in response.

"I'm going skiing ok? They are shutting the resort tomorrow so want to go up one last time. Let me know if you fancy joining us when you surface."

A mumble came out of her semi-comatose boyfriend before he turned over and went back to sleep.

Doubting he would have any recollection of what she had said, especially with the amount of alcohol coursing through his veins, she scribbled a note on a scrap piece of paper and propped it up next to the glass of water she had filled for him.

Once she scrabbled around for her clothing, delayed somewhat by her inability to locate her knickers and rogue ski sock, she got dressed and started walking home.

Half way back, she recognised the brunette head bobbing along in front of her.

"Oy! Michelle!" she hollered at the top of her voice. Her lack of hangover was amazing, she marvelled, as the volume of her voice failed to hurt her head. For once after a night out, she felt

170

great. The same could not be said for the peaky Michelle who turned around to greet her friend as she jogged to catch her up.

"Hello you dirty stop out, where were you last night?"

"Oh God, Eimear," Michelle moaned, "I feel like absolute shit. I think I am dying."

Eimear agreed that she looked like absolute shit too.

"Who?" she enquired nosily.

Michelle's alcohol-induced pale face flushed ever so slightly.

"I don't want to say."

"Aaaah! Ok! Jesus!" Michelle shrieked as Eimear dug her jokingly in the side, then caught her own head in her hands as the sound of her voice hurt it. "You are so mean when I am hungover, I am never this mean to you." She whined. Eimear thought otherwise but admitted this was perhaps not the time to debate it with her friend.

"It was Henry." Michelle whispered, too embarrassed to look Eimear in the eye.

Eimear's hand went straight to her mouth before she released a hugely undignified guffaw.

"Binky's Henry? I knew you would eventually!" She did a mini victory dance in the street. "I knew he would wear you down in the end!"

Henry had, in his defence, started a war of attrition against Michelle, and Eimear had been amazed that her friend had resisted him for so long.

"Yeah well, I bet he wished he hadn't bothered this morning," Michelle looked sheepish.

Eimear looked at her suspiciously. "What did you do?"

Her friend gulped before whispering, "I threw up on him. After, you know, we did it. It was all the rocking you see. Churned the drink up a bit."

Eimear had to take a moment to compose herself. She knew her friend needed her to say supportive but useless phrases like, "It will be fine" and "Oh, I'm sure he loved it really". However, she had to wait for the wave of hysteria to pass before she trusted herself to open her gob.

Michelle looked at her, rolled her eyes and nodded at her in what Eimear interpreted as a gesture giving her permission to laugh. She took the offer with much gusto and a good five minutes passed before she was able to dry her eyes and put together a full, coherent sentence.

"Well… at least he'll remember you." Was all she could come up with in the end.

"Great, thanks Emsie, that fills me with pride, it really does."

"Oh come on you," Eimear said as she linked arms with her friend and they started walking again. "It's nearly the end of the season and in only two weeks you will never have to see him again. It is a beautiful day, we don't have to start deep cleaning the chalet until tomorrow and everyone is heading up the slopes to enjoy the last day of skiing. Come with us, you'll feel better after a shower, food, ibuprofen and a good ski."

"There is no way I am skiing," Michelle grumbled. "I am going to bed where I can die from my hangover and shame in peace."

As they neared The Palace, Eimear could not help but chuckle to herself again. It was going to be a fun last two weeks.

CHAPTER 28

It was a miracle but somehow, Eimear managed to get Michelle up on the slopes with the rest of their team. Admittedly, it was not the best skiing her friend had ever done and there was a moment when Eimear feared Michelle would knock into a group of boarders resting beside the slope, sending them over the edge of the cliff. She definitely did not have good hand-eye-leg-ski co-ordination today. The real low point, however, was when she had to lean over the edge of the ski lift to puke as it dangled mid-air, much to the horror and disgust of the skiers and boarders on the piste below.

After a few more shady moments, Eimear conceded that Michelle was not going to get any better. She found her friend a sun lounger out the front of one of their favourite cafes where she could sleep whilst the rest of the group went off to do a few more runs.

Looking after Michelle was hardly a big ask she thought as she waved the rest of them off towards the nearest ski lift. She loved sunbathing on the slopes and knowing that it was possible to catch a decent tan whilst surrounded by snow still amazed her. Had anyone told her how hot it would get at the end of the season, she would have been convinced that they were taking her for a ride. But it was true. The majority of the snow in L'Homme had melted and some of the lower slopes in the ski resort had already been closed due to the lack of snow. It was quite scary actually, Eimear thought, seeing the rocks and shrubbery emerge from beneath the snow.

Had she known that's what she had been skiing over for the last few months, she wasn't sure she would have ever got onto a pair of skis. The slopes further up the mountain had remained open but even they were struggling for snow, using the fake snow cannons as regularly as possible.

There was a real party atmosphere in the resort now; many restaurants had live entertainment outside them and the restaurant the girls currently sat at had a saxophonist playing along to an array of music, from jazz to dance. People whizzed past them in short-sleeve t-shirts and hoodies tied around their waist. A few even resembled pandas, with tanned cheeks and huge white circles surrounding their eyes thanks to their ski goggles.

Eimear ordered the two of them cokes, then lay back in her recliner, put her sunglasses on and closed her eyes. This really was the life she decided as she felt the sun upon her face. When the cokes arrived, she put Michelle's drink on the table next to her now snoozing friend so it was within reach should she want it, then pulled out her book from the largest pocket within her salopettes and started reading. She relished the peace and quiet; she had not had much time to herself throughout the whole five months and sitting there reading her book in peace was a novelty.

Ok, so not quite alone, she thought as she glanced over at her friend. But she was borderline unconscious so it was as good as.

She was getting to a particularly good bit in her book when a familiar voice interrupted her.

"I thought I might find you here."

She was a bit surprised to find that it was not joy or excitement that flooded her as she laid eyes on her boyfriend, but irritation. She wasn't really in the mood for him right now, she just wanted to sit back and relax, read her book, then chill out with her friends when they returned.

But he had made the effort to come up to join them, she berated herself, so gave him a welcoming smile. Her book, she was sure, could wait.

He unclipped his skis, gave her a quick hello kiss and then took the seat beside her. He caught a waiter's eye and ordered some chips to help with the slight hangover he had. The moment the chips arrived, a tiny voice piped up, "Giz us a chip Ry, my stomach is in a state of mourning for all the food I've puked up."

Ryan rolled his eyes and good naturedly, moved over on his seat so Michelle could perch on the edge and tuck into his chips. Eimear smiled as she watched the two of them. She was lucky really, she had a lovely boyfriend and wonderful best friend. A best friend who just shoved too many chips inside her gob before spraying them all over her boyfriend's legs as she had a coughing fit.

Classy as always.

When Michelle composed herself, she asked Ryan if he was looking forward to returning to their homeland.

He took a second to respond, glancing over at Eimear before he said anything. "I am now. It has taken me a while to get used to the idea but I am really happy because I'll get to see my girl back at home now too. You are rank Michelle; get your slobber off of my legs now."

The two of them bantered while scoffing the rest of Ryan's chips so Eimear returned to her book. A second plate of chips arrived at Michelle's request but halfway through them, Michelle started to look a bit peaky again and headed off to the restaurant's toilets, leaving Ryan and Eimear alone.

"How are you doing my love?" he asked, reaching over and clasping her hand.

"I'm good thank you, enjoying the last day in the sun."

"Fancy a love ski in a bit, just you and me?"

"Definitely but I want to wait until the others are back so they can look after Drunky McShitfaced.

"Actually, great timing," she said as she started waving frantically in the direction of their friends who had just skied down the nearest slope. Once general chitchat finished, Eimear found that Emma wanted to head home so enlisted her to take Michelle back with her.

"Cool, thank you," Eimear said as she stood up and started collecting her stuff together. "Hey, Mitch, want to go home?"

A pale Michelle, who had just emerged from the depths of the restaurant, nodded. "Can someone take me home please, I fear I may not make it back alive if I go alone."

Emma laughed. "Come on you, you're with me. We'll see you guys later." She helped Michelle put her skis back on and then they skied off towards the lift which would take them home.

Eimear and Ryan clipped their skis back on and said their goodbyes while the rest of the group settled into the chairs they had just vacated.

"Where to?" Ryan asked as they looked at the various lifts available to them. Eimear had recently discovered a new red that she could do really well, in spite of the steep and narrow sections of the slope. She gestured to the lift which would take them up to it using her ski pole. "That one?"

"As you wish!" Ryan said and skated off towards the lift.

While they sat on the lift and were swung up to great heights through the air, Eimear took the opportunity to try and imprint the view on her memory. It really was breath-taking; she could see the snow-covered mountain tops for miles, some of which were now showing signs of beautiful foliage underneath. The sun sparkled on the snow and a river, recently unfrozen thanks to the changing season, flowed nearby.

"I really am going to miss this," she said before looking at Ryan. She wished she hadn't said anything; Ryan's face was twisted in fear and anger as he looked around at the scenery too. When he noticed she was looking at him, he attempted a smile.

"Me too." He said, before looking back out over the mountains in silence.

They reached the top of the lift, raised the bar and then skied off to the top of the red run. As Eimear started to go, she realised Ryan wasn't beside her. Looking around, she saw that he was standing at the top of the black run, which ran adjacent to the red piste.

"Come on," he said, gesturing to it.

"No way in hell," she said, backing away slightly. "Are you mad? I've made it this far through the season without killing myself, why would I risk dying now?"

Ryan grinned at her. "You're such an idiot. You can do it easily and you said you wanted to do a black run before you went home. I cannot let you back out of it now. Come on. I am going to be with you the whole time and will not let anything bad happen to you."

Eimear hesitated. It really would be a shame to go home without conquering one black...

Seeing her resolve breaking slightly, Ryan continued with his coaxing until she found herself at the top of the black run, looking over its steep edge. It wasn't any black run, but one with mounds of snow, known as moguls, on it.

She started to feel panicky. "Ryan, I don't know, I don't think I can do this," she stammered.

"Too late," he said as he gave her a gentle push, forcing her to go onto the slope. There was no turning back.

She started yelling every expletive she could muster at him.

"Spend less time swearing and more time turning!" he yelled back. "Bend your knees!"

There was nothing for it but for her to start bending and turning. Every now and then she would yell a little a reminder of how she was going to kill Ryan, followed by another expletive but the further she got down the slope, the less panicky she became. She hadn't fallen yet and, dare she admit it, she was actually enjoying herself. She stopped on the edge of the piste for a moment and looked up at the route she had just done. She could not believe her eyes. She was looking up at a sheer drop and she, the girl who was scared of everything, had just done it! Without dying!

With renewed confidence in her own abilities, she took off down the last part of the slope with flair and glee.

Ryan was waiting for her at the bottom and as he opened his arms to welcome her, she skied straight into them.

"I want you to know that officially, I am mad at you," she said, "But secretly, I am thrilled. Thank you."

"I knew you could do it, I am very proud of you. You're welcome," he replied, kissing her nose as he did. "Come on, let's go and tell the others what you have done."

As she watched him ski off in front of her, she felt her heart strings tug. She had not allowed herself to think about it too much but my God, she liked that guy. Dare she think it, she might even love him.

Pushing the thought away slightly, she took off after him, grinning from ear to ear at her achievement. What a way to end the skiing part of her season.

CHAPTER 29

While the party side of the end of season was amazing, the cleaning side was not. Each of them had to deep clean their chalet and the staff accommodation, a chore that required them to scrub every crevice, utensil, wall, floor, cupboard and surface. Doing it with hangovers, as most of them had every day, did not make it any easier. It did, however, help numb the pain of having to listen to Lucy and Ian every day, as they followed them around checking their every cleaning move.

"I never thought I would say this," Andrew reflected, elbow deep in a toilet, "but I am sincerely grateful to whichever of you bastards bought that last round of Jagerbombs last night because they have pretty much killed my senses. I can't even muster up the energy to pretend I am listening to those two anymore."

Instead of focusing on their own chalets separately, the couples had teamed together to tackle each of their chalets in turn. It seemed to make the job go much faster, as they divided up the chores amongst them and made what would be a miserably boring job far more enjoyable.

Eimear had volunteered to do the windows in what was Rory's and Ruth's chalet and was in the middle of scrubbing one of their downstairs windows when she spotted Ryan's mini-bus come screeching into the driveway. She saw him jump out of the driver's seat and, forgetting to close the door, race up to the front of the chalet whilst frantically trying to dial his mobile as he did. She got off the step ladder, put down her spray and newspaper, and went outside to meet him, feeling slightly worried at his erratic behaviour.

"Ryan!" she called to him. "I'm here, are you ok? You look a little bit deranged."

"Eimear!" he ran over to her, picked her up and spun her around.

"You never guess what! I have the best news ever!"

Laughing as he swung her around and steadying herself once

he put her down, it took her a moment or two before she enquired into his fantastic news.

"I don't have to go home!"

He started rambling on about how he had managed to secure a long-term job in L'Homme which meant he had work throughout the year so would have a steady source of income. He had spoken to his parents and they had acknowledged that is was a good job for him to do so they were no longer expecting him to give up his dream home and move back.

But Eimear heard none of it. It was as though someone had injected ice through her veins. The words "I don't have to go" kept racing around her brain but no matter how often she heard them, no matter how many times she tried, she could not quite see past them.

This could not be happening to her.

She tried to focus on him and his shocking declaration which had left her so cold but she could not escape the fear which had spread through her.

He didn't even seem to notice that she was stunned into silence, nor did he see the lack of colour in her face or her trembling body.

He skipped around her, rejoicing in his news.

"And it gets better! I have a job for you too! As part of the managerial role I get to choose both the hotel's summer and winter staff scheme so you have a job! You can waitress all year round! Isn't this great? It's not the end for us!"

Still she couldn't speak, too shocked and too heartbroken was she to stop his incessant monologue. She just stared at him, listening to him go on and on about this perfect future he saw for them both, him managing and her waitressing.

"I just want you to stay with me," he was saying. "I meant everything I said to you. I have never felt like this before. I actually love you so much. I know we haven't said the love thing yet but I want you to know it, it is true."

Thoughts of everything she had worked for flashed before her. The effort, blood, sweat and tears she had shed to ensure she got the best results possible so she could go to her first choice university. The pride she and her family had felt the day she had received her acceptance letter from University College Dublin. The excitement she felt regularly whenever she thought of going off to university in September, the people she would meet and the potential future she could have.

The fear she had felt at leaving her family for the first time and how delighted she was that, not only had she got through her ski season, she had done so without either killing herself or any of her guests. The excitement she had felt at going home, not only to her family but because she got to show off her boyfriend to them too. Her boyfriend. Her first ever boyfriend.

"So Eimear," Ryan looked at her at last. "Will you stay?" he looked so hopeful and did not even seem to notice the impact this announcement had made on her.

She couldn't speak, her breathing had increased so rapidly, it was hard to swallow, let alone comprehend everything he was saying to her.

She started recalling the beautiful times they had had together. The night he drove her to the top of the mountain peak to watch the sun set behind the snow-filled mountain tops; digging her van out of a snow drift after she had got it stuck for the umpteenth time to stop her getting yet another warning from her dictatorial bosses; holding her hair back for her after she had one Sambuca shot too many and had spent the rest of the night in her favourite position – naked using the toilet seat as a pillow.

He had insisted on finding her a rug to wrap around her goosepimple-filled body after she refused to remove her cheek from the cold plastic pillow; watching the meteor shower streak through the cloudless star-filled night; holding her close on a cold evening, sticking her freezing feet in between his warm thighs to stop her shivering body whilst whispering all of his dreams for their future together; the night he took her virginity, when he told her he would never let her go, that she would be his forever.

All of the memories, moments she had held so close to her

heart tainted the moment he uttered the fateful words, "I don't have to go home."

"So? Eimear? My love? Will you stay with me?"

It was over. They were over. The realisation of this hit her so hard and the pain which seared through her body was overwhelming.

Still words failed her, the pain and fear she was experiencing was so intense.

She looked back at the chalet where her friends, both new and old, worked together to get the chalets into some sort of shape. Inside, they were all discussing the next stage of their adventure, where they were going to go next and with whom. The most overriding conversation though, was everyone's excitement at going home, going back to their loved ones after five long months of being without them.

In that moment, she knew what she had to do. She turned and looked deeply into the hopeful, scared eyes of the first man she had ever loved, the man she had given herself to and in one word, broke his heart.

"No.

"Ryan, I do love you. I know I haven't said it before but I do. Perhaps it is just some whimsical, romantic holiday love but it is the only one I know for now. So I can say it with some certainty. But there is something else I do know with absolute conviction. This place is not my future; it is just somewhere I lived with my friend so I could learn something new, form good memories and go a little bit wild for a while. This place that you see as your future is soon to be my past. I have so much more I want to do with my life. I want to carry on travelling, I want to go to university but most importantly, I want to go home. I want to see my mum, my dad and my brothers.

"I can't stay here with you, Ryan. I am not throwing everything away just because I met some guy abroad. So no, my answer is no."

She started to walk away from him but he ran up to her and grabbed her.

"Eimear wait. You can't do this. I know you love this place,

I know you are sad to leave. You just said you love me didn't you? Well stay for me."

"I obviously don't love you enough. Now can you please go. I have work to do."

And with that, she turned her back on him and walked into the chalet, leaving him staring desolately at her retreating body.

CHAPTER 30

That last week was, emotionally, the hardest week of Eimear's life. The team were amazing and rallied around her as she tried to piece together her broken heart.

After turning Ryan down, she had locked herself in the bathroom of the chalet and sobbed until she thought she would make herself sick. When there were no tears left, she went and found Michelle who quickly took control. Getting someone to take over their jobs, she took Eimear back to the Palace, made her a cup of tea, ordered her to wash her face and then confiscated her mobile so, as would undoubtedly happen, the two could not make contact with each other when the urge came upon them.

They had seen Ryan around the town, as was to be expected in such a small place as L'Homme. But the guys had not let Ryan talk to her and the girls would whisk Eimear away so she would not be able to see him for long. She had received messages from him, both via her mobile and Facebook, begging her to give them a chance, either long distance or by doing another season. But when Michelle finally reunited her with her phone, Eimear did not respond to one of them, much to her amazement. She was proud of herself; she was not willing to sacrifice what she wanted from her life just because she had been besotted with some guy. His announcement had been the wake-up call she had needed and had confirmed what she had known to be true all along. She just had not been ready to believe it yet. They were never meant to survive outside of the ski resort. His was a fleeting love, one she would store in her memory, one day favourably she was sure, but for now all she could dwell on was the pain.

It was an odd mixture of relief and sadness she felt as she left L'Homme for the last time. As the van had driven away from the town, she had looked back out of the window of the mini-bus at the place she had called home. The grass, which had appeared yellow and lifeless thanks to the snow which had covered it for so long, had turned a luscious green and spring could be seen across the mountains. She smiled; beauty always followed, even when things appeared desolate.

Leaving the team at the airport as they all went off to their various departure gates had been really difficult. They had been so close throughout the season and it was really weird to think she may not ever see them again. She was really going to miss them.

Eimear leant her head against the plane window as she looked at the scenery below. The Irish landscape was so different from the environment she had become used to for the last five months. It was weird to be coming home.

As the plane dipped, she reflected on the five months and all she had achieved. She had loved and lost and survived them both. She learnt she was strong, independent and knew what she wanted to achieve from her not too distant future. She had not only successfully had sex but had managed to have it without getting pregnant or an STD. She had even managed to shake off some of the clutches of her Catholic guilt.

And most importantly, she had had the most amazing experience of her life.

By the time the plane screeched across the runway, she was hopeful. She would fall in love one day; she believed it would happen for her and next time, it would be for real and forever. But not yet. She did not want it yet. She had so much still to do, having a man in her life would just weigh her down.

Inside the baggage collection, she and Michelle pulled their various cases from the carousel and started dragging them out towards the arrivals gate.

"So," Michelle queried, "fancy America?" She turned to her friend with a huge grin on her face.

"You better believe it," Eimear responded, matching her friend's expression.

"Awesome. I'll call you in a few nights and we'll get planning ok?"

"Sounds like a plan to me. Hey, Michelle, I want to say bye to you now before we go through those doors because my mother is not going to give me a moment's peace the moment she sees me."

The two girls grinned and grabbed each other in a bear hug.

"It's been emotional," Eimear said.

"You're a knob, you know that?" Michelle responded, smacking her friend hard on the arm as she did.

"Come on, let's go."

And the two girls made their way through the arrivals gate, dragging the past five months in their cases behind them, towards their excited friends and family beyond.

ACKNOWLEDGEMENTS

There are so many people to whom I must give thanks for help-ing me throughout this process. Whether it was a gentle word of encouragement, a swift kick in the backside when I was slacking off or assiduously reading version after version, it has all helped me achieve my goal of becoming a published author.

Firstly, to my parents, Geraldine and Cillian. Thank you so much for giving me the love and encouragement to follow a dream. If you hadn't believed in me and let me be a bum for so long in our family home while I wrote, I would not have suc-ceeded.

To my little brother, Caolan. You have always been so enthusi-astic about every stage of this process. Whether it was just get-ting a chapter finished or hearing that the book was going to be published, I always knew I could depend on you to share in my joy and jump around the house like an excited moron.

My beloved Freyja. You accepted draft after draft without complaint and I always knew I could depend on you to answer WhatsApp messages, no matter what the hour, when I was hav-ing yet another crisis of confidence.

To Bethan, for telling me how far I could take the Catholicism and for reading the first ever version for me when I was most unsure.

To Grace, for helping me think up titles mid-squats at circuits and trying to work out what the 'done thing' at a book launch really was.

To all of my brilliant colleagues; thank you for setting much needed deadlines and for our brainstorming sessions. Your sup-port, enthusiasm and excitement has done so much for me, I can never completely express my gratitude.

To Jenna and Kirsty, for all of the post-book support they have given me, from spreading the word to helping with the book launch.

To Imogen, for saying 'yes' that day I asked if I could gate-crash your ski season. If it wasn't for you, I never would have been exposed to such an amazing world of snow, skiing, laughter and Jagerbombs.

To Alex at Silverdart, thank you for reading my blog on that snowy, grey day and telling me to get in touch if I wanted my stories to become something more. You turned a dream into a reality.

Finally, to Steve. You came into my life when I had already started writing and you just accepted this hope of mine. From the beginning, you have always believed it was possible and not a day has gone by without your support. Thank you for telling me to 'stop socialising and just get on with it'. Good words, I did just that.

Thank you all, I will be eternally grateful for your support.

Like the book?
Tell Danann @DanannSwanton or www.danannswanton.co.uk

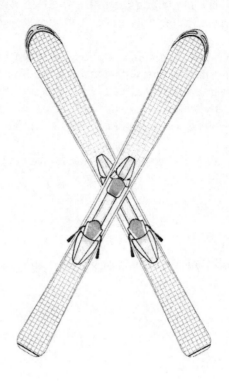